Pokémon™
ADVENTURES
BLACK & WHITE

9
VOLUME NINE
Story by
Hidenori Kusaka
Art by
Satoshi Yamamoto

& WHITE

SOME PLACE IN SOME TIME... A YOUNG TRAINER NAMED BLACK, WHO DREAMS OF WINNING THE POKÉMON LEAGUE, RECEIVES A POKÉDEX FROM PROFESSOR JUNIPER AND SETS OFF TO COLLECT THE EIGHT GYM BADGES HE NEEDS TO ENTER NEXT YEAR'S POKÉMON LEAGUE.

BLACK SUCCEEDS IN COLLECTING ALL EIGHT BADGES AT THE LAST MINUTE AND SUCCEEDS IN DEFEATING HIS OPPONENTS TO MOVE UP INTO THE FINALS. BUT HIS OPPONENT IN THE FINAL MATCH, CHEREN, HAS BEEN STRONGLY INFLUENCED BY TEAM PLASMA.

MEANWHILE, WHITE REALIZES THAT GRAY AND HOOD MAN WERE MEMBERS OF TEAM PLASMA, BUT SHE IS KIDNAPPED BY HOOD MAN.

BLACK MANAGES TO DEFEAT CHEREN AMIDST THE CHAOTIC SITUATION, AND HIS ANGER TOWARDS TEAM PLASMA FOR USING HIS FRIEND AWAKENS RESHIRAM FROM THE LIGHT STONE!

A STORY ABOUT YOUNG PEOPLE ENTRUSTED WITH POKÉDEXES BY THE WORLD'S LEADING POKÉMON RESEARCHERS. TOGETHER WITH THEIR POKÉMON, THEY TRAVEL, BATTLE, AND EVOLVE!

WHITE

THE PRESIDENT OF BW AGENCY. HER DREAM IS TO DEVELOP THE CAREERS OF POKÉMON STARS. SHE TAKES HER WORK VERY SERIOUSLY AND WILL DO WHATEVER IT TAKES TO SUPPORT HER POKÉMON ACTORS.

LOOKER

AN INTERNATIONAL POLICE INVESTIGATOR. HE IS AFTER THE SEVEN SAGES OF TEAM PLASMA AND IS CONDUCTING AN UNDERCOVER INVESTIGATION AT THE POKÉMON LEAGUE.

PROFESSOR JUNIPER (FATHER)

PROFESSOR JUNIPER'S FATHER. HE IS A RENOWNED POKÉMON RESEARCHER IN THE UNOVA REGION. HE IS KEEPING AN EYE ON TEAM PLASMA FROM THE POKÉMON LEAGUE STADIUM.

POKÉMON ADVENTURES The Tenth Chapter 10 BLACK

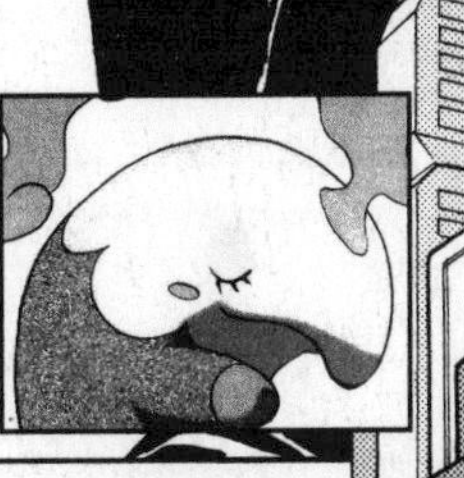

PLACE: UNOVA REGION

A HUGE AREA FULL OF MODERN CITIES, MANY OF WHICH ARE CONNECTED TO EACH OTHER BY BRIDGES. RISING FROM THE CENTER OF THE REGION ARE THE SKYSCRAPERS OF CASTELIA CITY, UNOVA'S URBAN CENTER.

BLACK

A TRAINER WHOSE DREAM IS TO WIN THE POKÉMON LEAGUE. A PASSIONATE YOUNG MAN WHO, ONCE HE SETS OUT TO ACCOMPLISH SOMETHING, CAN'T BE STOPPED. HE ALSO DOES HIS RESEARCH AND PLANS AHEAD. HE HAS SPECIAL DEDUCTIVE SKILLS THAT HELP HIM ANALYZE INFORMATION TO SOLVE MYSTERIES.

GHETSIS

LEADER OF THE SEVEN SAGES. HE SPEAKS OF POKÉMON LIBERATION AND SCHEMES TO MAKE AN ATTACK ON THE POKÉMON LEAGUE...

N

THE KING OF TEAM PLASMA. HE AWAKENED ZEKROM FOR HIS "IDEAL"...

HOOD MAN

A MYSTERIOUS TRAINER. HE SEEMS TO BE COOPERATING WITH TEAM PLASMA, BUT WHY?!

GRAY (ZINZOLIN)

HIS TRUE IDENTITY IS ZINZOLIN OF THE SEVEN SAGES. HE HAS POISONED CHEREN'S MIND TO GIVE HIM A COLD HEART.

POKÉMON™ ADVENTURES BLACK & WHITE

9 VOLUME NINE

CONTENTS

KELDEO

Adventure 59
Something Suspicious

YOU THINK WE WEREN'T INVITED TO THE BATTLE AT THE NACRENE MUSEUM BECAUSE THE OTHERS BELIEVE WE'RE TOO **WEAK**?!
THAT WE HAVE TO GANG UP TOGETHER JUST TO PROTECT A SINGLE GYM?
THAT THE THREE OF US DON'T EVEN EQUAL ONE GYM LEADER?!
HEH HEH HEH...

LISTEN UP! WE ARE SO STRONG THAT—
IT'S POINTLESS TO ARGUE WITH THEM, CHILI.
THEY'LL SOON FIND OUT HOW "WEAK" WE ARE— WHEN WE **FIGHT** THEM!

tooo
Shh
thud
thwap
thwap
thwap
thwap

THEIR POKÉMON TYPES ARE AT A DISADVANTAGE, BUT THEY'VE TURNED THINGS AROUND!
HUH ?!

CON-GRATU-LA-TIONS, YOU THREE!
WHEN WE WERE APPOINTED GYM LEADERS OF STRIATON CITY, LENORA TOLD US...
THAT'S RIGHT!
TYPE ADVAN-TAGES...
THAT'S THE REASON THE THREE OF US PROTECT THE SAME GYM!

YOUR GYM HAS BEEN SPECIALLY DESIGNED TO TEACH TRAINERS ABOUT ***TYPE ADVANTAGES.***
NOW, JUST BECAUSE YOU'RE IN CHARGE OF ONE POKÉMON GYM DOESN'T MEAN YOU AREN'T AS GOOD AS THE OTHER GYM LEADERS...

HOLD YOUR HEAD UP HIGH! TAKE PRIDE IN YOUR ROLE!
WE NEED A GYM THAT TEACHES TRAINERS ABOUT TYPES—AND THAT'S WHERE ***YOU*** COME IN!
pof

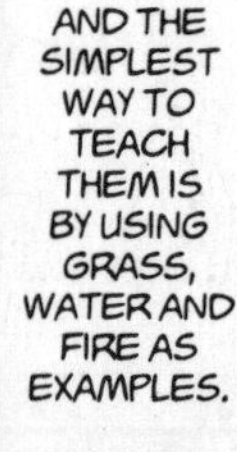

TYPE ADVAN-TAGES ARE THE FIRST THING A ROOKIE TRAINER NEEDS TO KNOW.
AND THE SIMPLEST WAY TO TEACH THEM IS BY USING GRASS, WATER AND FIRE AS EXAMPLES.

GRASS IS STRONG AGAINST WATER. WATER IS STRONG AGAINST FIRE. AND FIRE IS STRONG AGAINST GRASS.
IT'S WHAT YOU'D CALL A THREE-WAY STAND-OFF... KIND OF LIKE ROCK, PAPER, SCISSORS.

WOULDJA LIKE TO BATTLE ME TO SEE HOW STRONG I AM, LENORA?
THAT'S RIGHT!
EACH OF US IS AN OFFICIAL GYM LEADER!
YES!
HA HA HA! YOU DON'T HAVE TO PROVE ANYTHING TO ME! AND IT LOOKS LIKE YOU HAVE THINGS UNDER CONTROL.

SO MAYBE YOU SHOULD GIVE SOME THOUGHT AS TO WHY WE'RE HERE, HUH...?
WHAT?

YOU...
...FOLLOWED US?!

EXACTLY!
AND THAT'S NOT ALL! WE'RE ALSO LOOKING FOR THESE!
...!

LEAF STONE!
WATER STONE!
FIRE STONE!

Snag
Snag
Snag
Snag

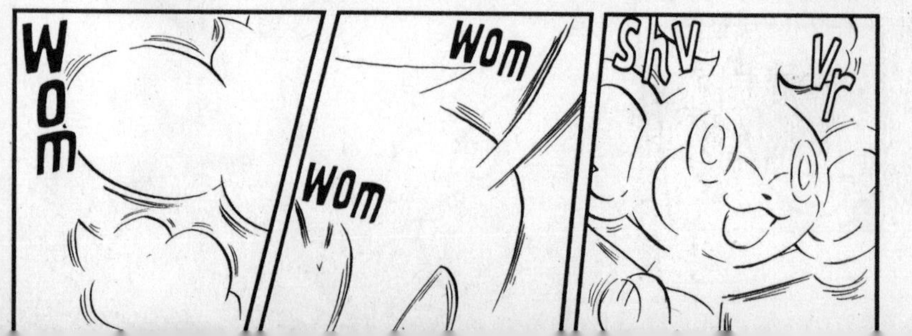
Wom
Wom
Wom
Shv
Vr

WOM
snap
splash
foo
sh

H

IT'S JUST AS I ANTICIPATED... THE HUMANS HAVE BEGUN AN UGLY BATTLE.
TAKE A GOOD LOOK, KELDEO.

WHICH OF THEM IS IN THE WRONG?

KRES

THERE'S NO SUCH THING AS RIGHT OR WRONG IN A BATTLE BETWEEN HUMANS.
THEIR BATTLES ARE ALL ABOUT ***REJECTING*** EACH OTHER. THAT'S WHY THEY'RE SO HORRIBLE.

THEIR SKILLS...

THIS SIDE LOOKS STRONGER.

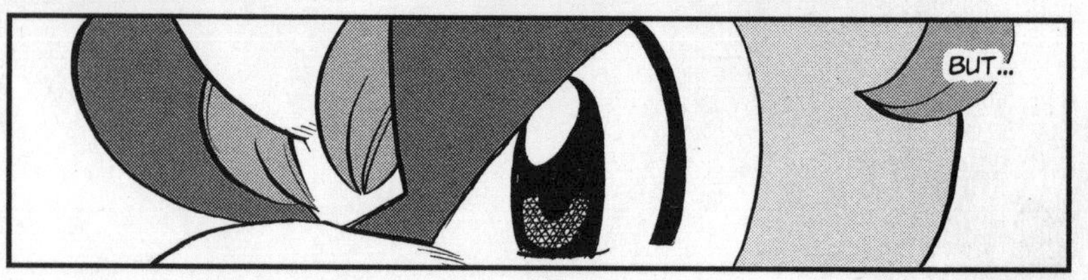
BUT...

EVEN THOUGH THEIR POKÉMON ARE FOLLOWING THEIR ORDERS...

...AND THEY'RE WINNING...

...THEY DON'T SEEM TO BE FIGHTING WITH ALL THEIR HEART. WHY IS THAT...?

I THINK IT'S BECAUSE... THEY DON'T WANT TO FIGHT THIS BATTLE. AND THEY'RE BEING FORCED TO FIGHT IN A WAY THEY DON'T LIKE.
THEY'RE SCARED OF *LOSING*! THAT'S WHAT IT IS! THEY'RE SCARED OF HOW THEIR TRAINERS WILL TREAT THEM IF THEY LOSE!

THEY'RE ENJOYING THEMSELVES! THEY'RE FULL OF LIFE.

THEIR MOVES AREN'T AS EFFECTIVE. BUT...

THE POKÉMON ON THIS SIDE ARE LOSING.

AND THAT'S NOT ALL!

THEIR EXPRESSIONS, EYES, VOICES, WORDS...
THESE POKÉMON'S TRAINERS CARE ABOUT HOW THEY FEEL. SO THE POKÉMON ARE GIVING THIS BATTLE THEIR ALL. THEY WANT TO DO WHAT HUMANS ASK OF THEM— TO PLEASE THEM.

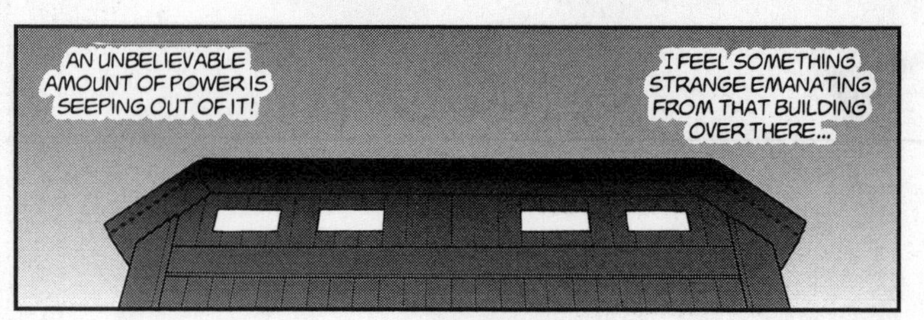
I FEEL SOMETHING STRANGE EMANATING FROM THAT BUILDING OVER THERE...
AN UNBELIEVABLE AMOUNT OF POWER IS SEEPING OUT OF IT!

IT DOESN'T FEEL RIGHT. AND THOSE PEOPLE...
...ARE GIVING OFF THAT SAME WEIRD FEELING!

IS THIS WHAT CO-BALION...
...WAS TALKING ABOUT?
BUT IT'S HUMANS LIKE THEM, WHO FORGET THEIR PLACE... ...THAT DO THINGS TO ENDANGER POKÉMON.

IS THERE REALLY NO SUCH THING AS GOOD AND BAD WHEN IT COMES TO HUMANS?

NO!
I THINK SOME HUMANS ARE DOING RIGHT AND SOME ARE DOING WRONG! AND I CHOOSE...
klomp

jump

WHAT ARE YOU DOING, KELDEO?!
PLEASE...
GIVE ME...
...PERMISSION!

PERMIS-SION TO USE MY SWORD!

...GO AHEAD.

shing
boing
tmp
WHAT THE–?!

SWISH
WHAT IS THAT POKÉMON ?!
IT'S HELP- ING US?!
slash
HEY!
WHEN DID YOU CALL OUT ANOTHER POKÉMON ...?

TMP
SM
OOSH
WFFF
KLOMP

AMAZ-ING!
IT DE-FEATED ALL OF THEM ALL BY ITSELF!
smak
I'VE ENDED...
...THIS BAT-TLE!
yank
NOW THAT IS A POWERFUL POKÉMON.
ATTACK IT WITH ALL YOUR MIGHT...
...AND CAP-TURE IT!
DON'T LET THEM CAPTURE THAT POKÉMON!
PRO-TECT IT!
thud

YOU LOST FOCUS AGAIN.
BUT YOUR USE OF SECRET SWORD WAS QUITE IMPRESSIVE.
SNKK

REMEMBER THIS, KELDEO...
YOU MUST NOT WIELD YOUR SWORD HALF-HEARTEDLY.

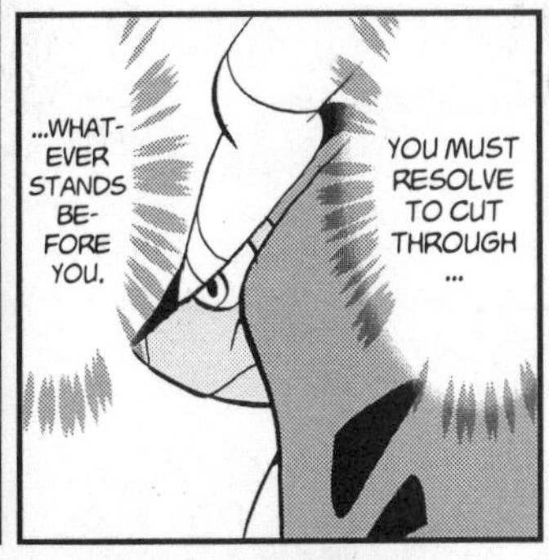
YOU MUST RESOLVE TO CUT THROUGH...
...WHATEVER STANDS BEFORE YOU.

"RESOLUTION"...

THERE IS ONE MORE "SWORD" TO WIELD...
...AND THAT WEAPON IS CALLED "RESOLUTION."

COBALION! LET'S DRIVE THESE HUMANS AWAY!
YES, LET'S!

shi
iii
iii
nnngg

thud

FALL BACK!
THEY'RE ABOUT TO USE A VERY POWER-FUL MOVE ...!

KA

HUMANS...
IF YOU EVER SET
FOOT IN THIS
PLACE AGAIN...

...YOUR
CLOTHES
...
...WON'T BE THE
ONLY THING I
DESTROY!

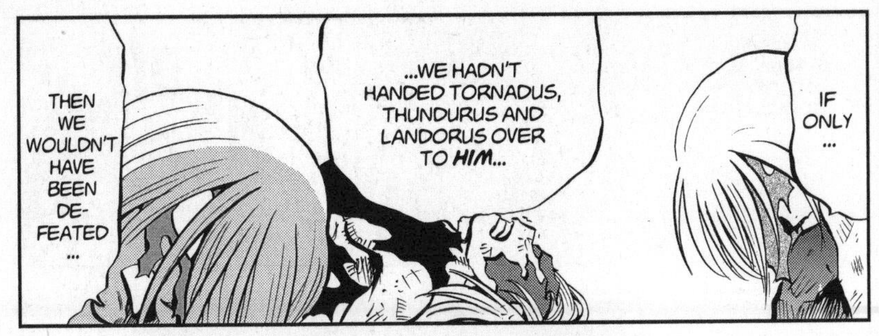
IF ONLY...
...WE HADN'T HANDED TORNADUS, THUNDURUS AND LANDORUS OVER TO HIM...
THEN WE WOULDN'T HAVE BEEN DE-FEATED...

WE'RE COMING BACK TO FINISH THIS... AS SOON AS THE RESEARCH ON HOW TO TURN THEM BACK INTO THEIR THERIAN FORMES...
...IS COM-PLETED!

WE DON'T HAVE TIME TO WAIT FOR THAT!
OUR OPERATION HAS ENTERED ITS FINAL PHASE!

HOW CAN WE FACE MASTER GHETSIS IF WE LET OUR ENEMIES WANDER AROUND WILLY-NILLY?
WAIT!
stggr
DON'T TELL ME YOU'RE GOING TO USE THAT!

ONLY FOR A MOMENT...
TO TEACH THEM A LESSON...

klak
GO!
r mbl
klang
klang

klaang
ANCIENT HUNTER!

foooom

WZZZZZZZZZ
HUH?
KELDEO!
LOOK OUT!

KRCCCK

splash
YOU ...
brrbl brrbl

ZEKROM VS RESHIRAM I

Adventure 60
Cold Hard Truth

sh
tnk
THUMP

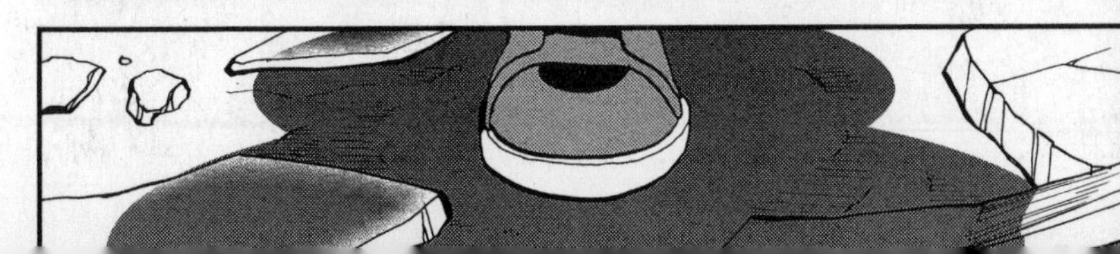

WON-
DER-
FUL!

THE
LIGHT
STONE...
...HAS
ANSWERED
YOUR CALL
AND
TRANS-
FORMED
BACK INTO
RESHIRAM.

GRAY!
WAIT... NO!
I REMEMBER
YOU NOW! YOU'RE
ZINZOLIN, ONE OF
THE SEVEN SAGES
OF TEAM
PLASMA!

HOW
DARE
YOU
MESS
WITH MY
FRIEND'S
HEAD!

FIRST,
PERMIT
ME TO
CON-
GRATU-
LATE
YOU.
YOUR
DREAM
HAS
JUST
BEEN
FUL-
FILLED.

rttl
rttl
rttl

KIKKIKIK

YOU HAVE WON THE POKÉMON LEAGUE!
AL-THOUGH ...
SADLY, THERE ARE NO SPECTATORS HERE TO APPLAUD YOUR VICTORY...

DON'T WORRY! MAYOR DRAYDEN AND IRIS HAVE EVACUATED EVERYBODY OUTSIDE!
WE WERE PRE-PARED FOR THIS!
THAT'S A RE-LIEF!
NOW I CAN FIGHT AS ROUGH AS I WANT!
krnch

WHERE ARE THE GYM LEADERS ?!
AND WHERE DID HOOD MAN TAKE MY BOSS?!
grab

WHITE?
CAN YOU HEAR ME, WHITE?

IT'S NO GOOD.
I'M NOT GETTING AN ANSWER FROM WHITE'S XTRANSCEIVER.

THE LAST CALL I GOT FROM HER WAS TO TELL ME THAT HOOD MAN AND GRAY SEEMED TO BE CONSPIRING WITH EACH OTHER... SHE SAID SHE WAS GOING TO MOVE CLOSER TO HEAR WHAT THEY WERE SAYING, AND THEN... NOTHING.
WHAT'S HAPPENED TO HER?!

AND WHAT...

...IS THE MEANING OF ***THIS***?!
tmp

I DUG UNDERGROUND BECAUSE I FELT...
...A STRANGE RESONANCE FROM BELOW THE POKÉMON LEAGUE STADIUM.

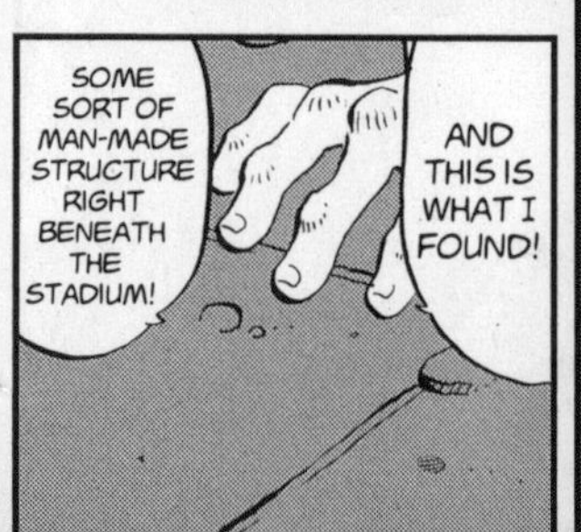
AND THIS IS WHAT I FOUND!
SOME SORT OF MAN-MADE STRUCTURE RIGHT BENEATH THE STADIUM!

shing
HUH?!
WHAT A SURPRISE!
I DIDN'T THINK ANYONE WOULD NOTICE.
I THOUGHT ALL YOU GYM LEADERS WERE PITIFUL DUNCES.
BUT I GUESS THERE ARE A FEW WHO STILL HAVE THEIR WITS ABOUT THEM.
HA HA HA! WHAT A SURPRISE!

TEAM PLASMA!
jingl
ARGH! IT'S ME, HAWES! I'M HERE TOO!
I'M LENORA'S HUSBAND!
!

WELCOME, BRYCEN.

GHET-SIS ...!
WELCOME ...
...TO OUR CASTLE.

THE GYM LEADERS ARE BEING HELD CAPTIVE INSIDE TEAM PLASMA'S CASTLE?! WHERE IS IT?!
YOUR... CASTLE ?!

HEY! WHAT WAS THAT?!
KLKK
RELAX... I'LL TAKE YOU THERE NOW.

IN A WAY, YES...
A RE-MOTE ...?
RMBL
RMBL
YOU JUST SIGNALED THE OTHER TEAM PLASMA MEMBERS, DIDN'T YOU?!

krkk krkk krkk

KABOOM

rmm
rmm
rmm
rmm
rmm

rm r mm m
rm m m
Shkk
rmmm m
SHNNNNK

UD

KATH

THIS ISN'T TEAM PLASMA'S CASTLE EXACTLY....
IT BE-LONGS TO OUR KING...

...TO N.

rmbl
rmbl
rmbl
rmbl

shk

dadunk

EEEEEEK!
AAAH!
sha

SMASSH

IRIS! ARE ALL THE SPECTA-TORS ALL RIGHT?!

I DON'T KNOW! I BROUGHT THEM OUTSIDE, BUT...
...I'M NOT SURE THAT WAS SUCH A GOOD IDEA!

EEK!
WHY? WHAT'S WRONG, IRIS?!
IT'S TEAM PLAS–
KZZT

SHING

LOOKS LIKE THE STAGE HAS BEEN SET...
IT'S ALL JUST AS MY FATHER ENVI-SIONED...

WAS THIS THE RIGHT THING TO DO, ANTHEA?
CON-COR-DIA?
THERE'S NO NEED FOR YOU TO WORRY, N.
EVERYTHING WILL WORK OUT AS PLANNED...

I SUPPOSE SO...
LET'S GO!
YOUR OPPOSITE HAS ALSO AWAKENED, ZEKROM.

ROOOAAARRR
RESHIRAM!
AND IT HAS NOTICED...
...THAT OUR KING IS ABOUT TO MAKE HIS ENTRANCE!
N!
THAT'S RIGHT...

ACK!

MR. HAWES!
FUMP
LONG TIME NO SEE, BLACK.

BRYCEN FOUND US. BUT HE GOT CAUGHT BECAUSE OF ME...

WE HAVE PROVEN OUR WORTH BY DEFEATING THE CHAMPION AND TAKING OVER THE POKÉMON LEAGUE!
BUT... THAT'S STILL NOT ENOUGH TO SPREAD OUR IDEAL...

OUR PLAN WILL ONLY BE COMPLETE AFTER WE SHOW EVERYONE THAT THEIR GYM LEADERS ARE POWERLESS.
THE SYMBOL OF THEIR TOWNS, THE GUARDIANS OF THE GYM BADGES, THEIR IDOLS...

BEHOLD ...
...THESE HELPLESS GYM LEADERS!

FUUFFF

flap

AND NOW THEY'RE MOCKING US! ARE YOU STILL UNWILLING TO STAND UP TO THEM?!

THEY'VE GONE A LITTLE TOO FAR IN THEIR CAMPAIGN TO SHARE THEIR BELIEFS...
IF I WERE TO WRITE A NOVEL ABOUT THIS, THIS WOULD BE WHERE THE CLIMACTIC BATTLE BEGINS!

GRIMS-LEY?!

...
SHAUNTAL, GET YOUR GOLURK OUT...
Snap

fooosh

HOOD MAN ?!
!
bampf

SINCE I'VE COME TO THE POKÉMON LEAGUE, I'VE GROWN CURIOUS. I'D LIKE TO SEE...
...HOW EACH OF THE ELITE FOUR DRAWS OUT THE STRENGTH OF THEIR POKÉMON...

BOM
BOM
BOM

THE LEGENDARY POKÉMON?!
YOU TAKE CARE OF THESE...
I'LL GO AFTER HIM!
GRIMSLEY!

THOSE THREE POKÉMON ARE IN THEIR INCARNATE FORMES NOW.
IT WOULD BE INTER-ESTING TO TEST THEIR POTENTIAL HERE...

I ALREADY KNOW HOW TO CHANGE THEM INTO THEIR THERIAN FORME.
ALL THAT'S LEFT IS... HEH HEH HEH HEH...

HA HA HA... YOU CAN'T DECIDE, CAN YOU?
WHETHER TO FLY UP AND FIGHT OUR KING OR TO SAVE THOSE RIDICULOUS GYM LEADERS?
BUT THE FACT IS...

...NEITHER OF THOSE ACTIONS ...
...ARE OP-TIONS.

EVEN THOUGH YOU HAVE YOUR "TRUTH"...

...IT SEEMS RESHIRAM HAS NO NEED FOR YOU ANYMORE NOW THAT IT HAS BEEN AWAKENED FROM ITS STONE.

THE OTHER GYM LEADERS ARE BUSY PROTECT-ING THE SPECTA-TORS...

THE CHAM-PION HAS MADE A RUN FOR IT AND IS NOWHERE TO BE FOUND...

AND THE ELITE FOUR HAVE THEIR HANDS FULL WITH THE THREE LEGENDARY POKÉMON...

THERE IS NO ONE LEFT HERE...
...WITH THE POWER TO STOP TEAM PLASMA!
WHAT MAKES YOU THINK...

...ONLY A CHAMP-PION...
...OR THE ELITE FOUR...
...OR THE GYM LEAD-ERS...
...CAN FACE YOU?!

WE ALL...
...HAVE A DREAM!
WE ALL LOVE POKÉMON!
WE ALL HAVE WHAT IT TAKES!

WHAT...
...THE?

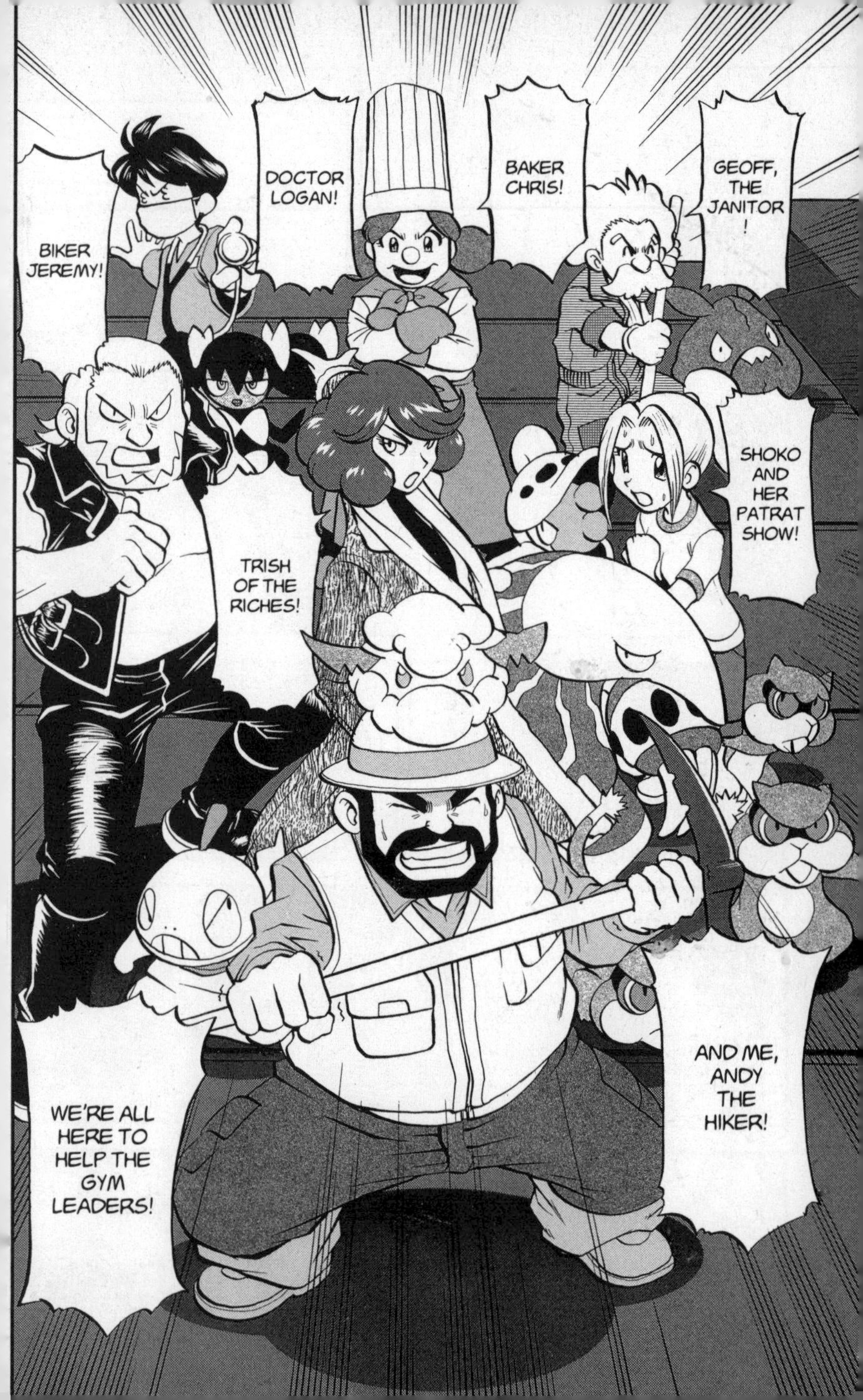
BIKER JEREMY!
DOCTOR LOGAN!
BAKER CHRIS!
GEOFF, THE JANITOR!
SHOKO AND HER PATRAT SHOW!
TRISH OF THE RICHES!
AND ME, ANDY THE HIKER!
WE'RE ALL HERE TO HELP THE GYM LEADERS!

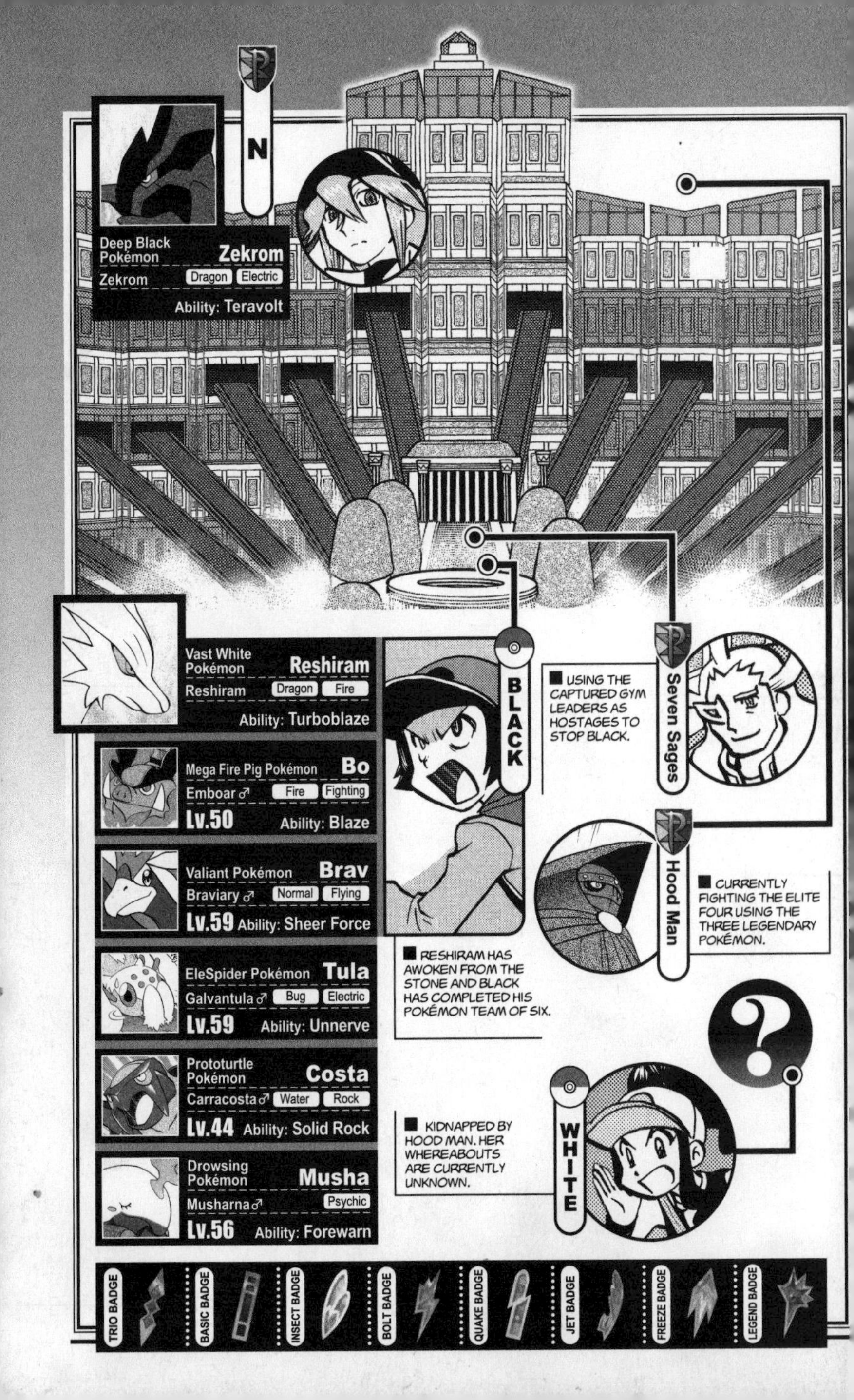
N
Deep Black Pokémon
Zekrom
Zekrom
Dragon
Electric
Ability: Teravolt
Vast White Pokémon
Reshiram
Reshiram
Dragon
Fire
Ability: Turboblaze
Mega Fire Pig Pokémon
Bo
Emboar ♂
Fire
Fighting
Lv.50
Ability: Blaze
Valiant Pokémon
Brav
Braviary ♂
Normal
Flying
Lv.59
Ability: Sheer Force
EleSpider Pokémon
Tula
Galvantula ♂
Bug
Electric
Lv.59
Ability: Unnerve
Prototurtle Pokémon
Costa
Carracosta ♂
Water
Rock
Lv.44
Ability: Solid Rock
Drowsing Pokémon
Musha
Musharna ♂
Psychic
Lv.56
Ability: Forewarn
BLACK
RESHIRAM HAS AWOKEN FROM THE STONE AND BLACK HAS COMPLETED HIS POKÉMON TEAM OF SIX.
Seven Sages
USING THE CAPTURED GYM LEADERS AS HOSTAGES TO STOP BLACK.
Hood Man
CURRENTLY FIGHTING THE ELITE FOUR USING THE THREE LEGENDARY POKÉMON.
WHITE
KIDNAPPED BY HOOD MAN. HER WHEREABOUTS ARE CURRENTLY UNKNOWN.
TRIO BADGE
BASIC BADGE
INSECT BADGE
BOLT BADGE
QUAKE BADGE
JET BADGE
FREEZE BADGE
LEGEND BADGE

Pokémon™
ADVENTURES
BLACK & WHITE
ZEKROM
VS
RESHIRAM
II
Adventure 61
Triple Threat

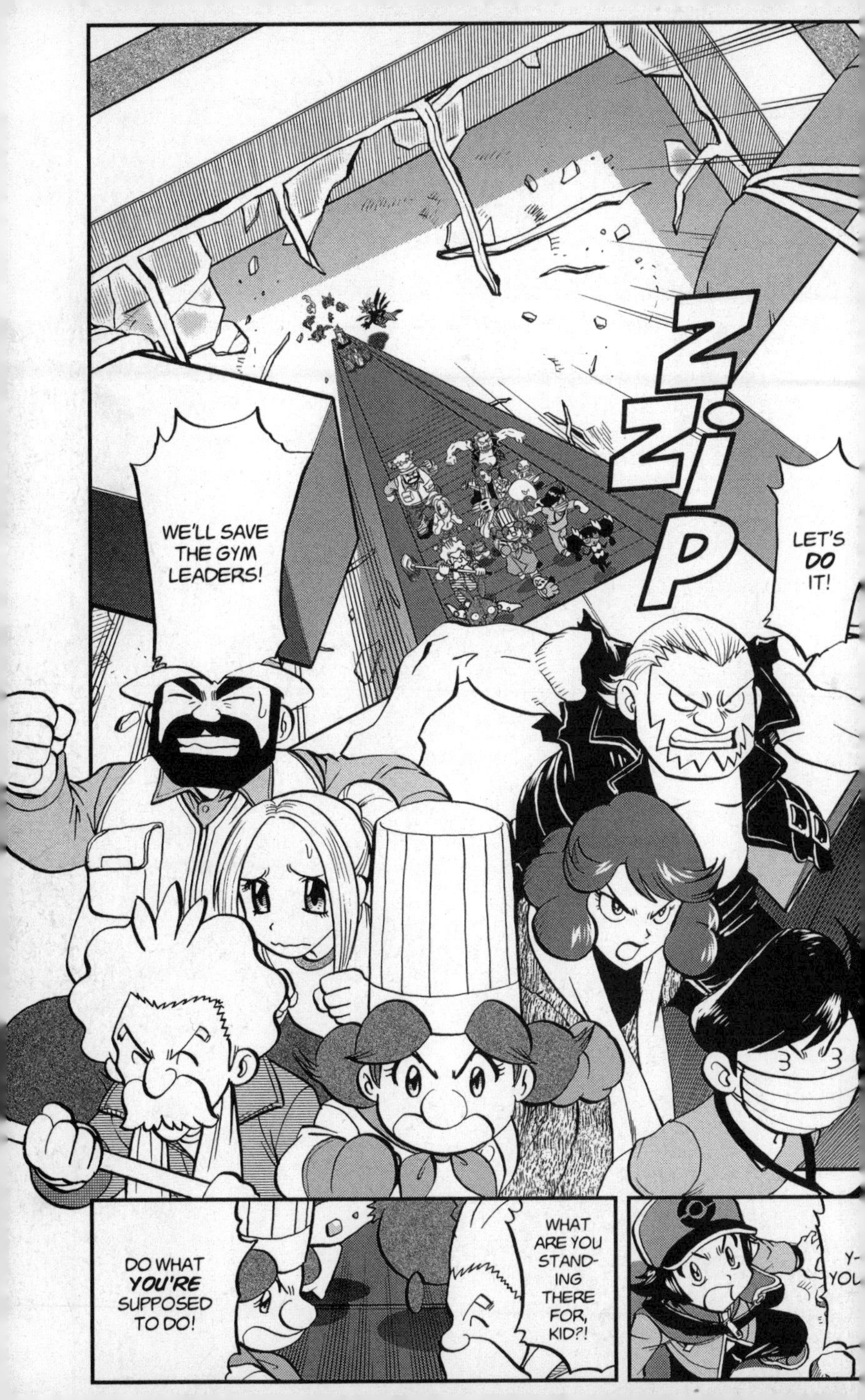
ZZIP
LET'S DO IT!
WE'LL SAVE THE GYM LEADERS!
Y-YOU
WHAT ARE YOU STANDING THERE FOR, KID?!
DO WHAT YOU'RE SUPPOSED TO DO!

THAT'S RIGHT, YOUNG MAN...
GO AND FACE YOUR TRUE OPPONENT!

DO... WHAT? WHAT AM I SUP-POSED TO...?
MY... TRUE OPPO-NENT...

TAKE ME TO RESHI-RAM!
BRAV!
SLOOP

RMBL
RMBL
RMBL
RMBL
TWO DRAGON-TYPE POKÉMON ARE ABOUT TO FIGHT!
murmur
murmur
IT'S JUST LIKE THE LEGEND OF THE CRE-ATION OF UNOVA!

THAT'S RIGHT!
TODAY IS THE DAY WE CELEBRATE... THE ***NEW*** CREATION OF UNOVA!

THE ONE WITH THE BLACK DRAGON-TYPE POKÉMON...
...IS OUR KING, THE HERO OF IDEALS!

...
WHO DO YOU THINK WILL WIN?
gulp
I DON'T KNOW...

I THINK RESHI-RAM IS GONNA WIN.

NO! ZEKROM!
I'M BET-TING ON RESHI-RAM!

WO
O
T
RO
OA AR
ZEK-ROM!
RESHI-RAM!
ZEK-ROM!
RESHI-RAM!
ZEK-ROM!
ZEK-ROM!
ZEK-ROM!
RESHI-RAM!
ZEK-ROM!
OH...
THE BATTLE BETWEEN THE "IDEAL" AND THE "TRUTH" IS NOTHING BUT...
RE-SHI-RAM!
...AN ENTER-TAINMENT TO THESE COMMON PEOPLE!
ZEK-ROM!
HOW SAD.
RESHI-RAM!
HOW VERY SAD.

THAT'S WHAT COMMON FOLK ARE LIKE. AND THAT'S WHY WE MUST LEAD THEM IN THE RIGHT DIRECTION.
AND TO ACCOMPLISH THAT, WE FIRST MUST GET RID OF THOSE...
...WHO WOULD MISLEAD THEM...
M-MAS-TER GHET-SIS...

I SHALL OVERLOOK YOUR DISOBEDIENCE AND INSUB-ORDINATION...
...BE-CAUSE NOW YOU MUST *FIGHT*!

LUNGE

GRRR!
NO SWEAT! THERE ARE SEVEN OF THEM AND SEVEN OF US! WE AREN'T OUT-NUMBERED!

THAT'S RIGHT!
CLEAR SMOG!
fwufff
foom
foom
NOT SO FAST...! USE HEX!!
smash
smash
BO, COSTA, MUSHA, TULA! GO AND HELP ANDY AND THE OTHERS!
BOM
BOM
BOM
BOM
BOM
T-TMP

TAKE A LOOK AT N.

DON'T WORRY, BRAV.

THANK YOU, YOUNG MAN!

HE'S ONLY GOT ZEKROM.
HE DOESN'T HAVE ANY OTHER POKÉMON WITH HIM EITHER.

ZIOOP
THIS MEANS ...
...IT'S GOING TO BE A ONE-ON-ONE BATTLE!

AND NOW, THE TWO LEGENDARY POKÉMON ARE ABOUT TO BATTLE AGAIN!
ru
mb
bl
SO...
...THIS IS IT, HUH?
I CAN'T STOP SHAK-ING...
I JUST ...
...CAN'T BE-LIEVE IT!
HERE I AM WITH LEGENDARY POKÉMON RESHIRAM...
...FACING OFF AGAINST LEGENDARY POKÉMON ZEKROM!

HIGH ABOVE THE POKÉMON LEAGUE STADIUM...
rmbl
rmbl

ZEKROM IS BEING RIDDEN BY MY ENEMY, N!
I HAVE TO FIGHT THEM BOTH TOGETH-ER!

AND TO TOP IT OFF...
URGH...
KRUSH

...THE ENERGY EMA-NATING FROM THESE TWO POKÉ-MON...
...IS TAKING A BIG TOLL ON ME!

BE CARE-FUL...
IF YOU CAN'T HEAR THE VOICE OF YOUR FRIEND RESHIRAM...

...YOU'LL BE CRUSHED FLAT.

WHOA!
lunge

WZZZ
ZOOP

FOOOM
FSSS

KOFF KOFF!
A DIRECT HIT! DID WE DO IT?

IS THAT THE BEST YOU CAN DO...?

JUST AS I THOUGHT ...
...YOU CAN'T HEAR RESHIRAM'S VOICE, CAN YOU?

GRRR !

WZZ
ZZZZZ
AAAH!

NUTS! ALL I'M DOING IS HOLDING ON TO RESHIRAM FOR DEAR LIFE! I HAVEN'T GIVEN ANY COMMANDS!

HEY, RESHIRAM ...
WHAT DO YOU NEED FROM ME?!
Krash
BLACK ...!

BLACK'S HAVING TROUBLE DRAWING OUT RESHIRAM'S FULL POWER.
I MIGHT BE ABLE TO ADVISE HIM...
IF ONLY I HAD THE MEANS TO FLY UP TO HIM!
ARE YOU IN NEED OF ASSISTANCE?
ALLOW ME TO HELP!
INTERNATIONAL POLICE EQUIPMENT: MIMIC BALLOON TYPE F!
OH!
YOU'RE A MEMBER OF THE INTERNATIONAL POLICE!
HUH?
HOW COULD HE TELL?!
NO! NOT AT ALL! I'M LOU KARR, YOUR EVERYDAY POKÉMON LEAGUE CONTESTANT! AHAHAHA...
BUT YOU—
ARE YOU GETTING INTO THE BALLOON OR NOT?!

HEY!
WAIT FOR ME!
I WANNA GO TOO!
LEO?!
I WANT TO CHEER BLACK ON!
THERE'S NO ROOM!
jump
WE'RE COMING TO HELP YOU, BLACK!

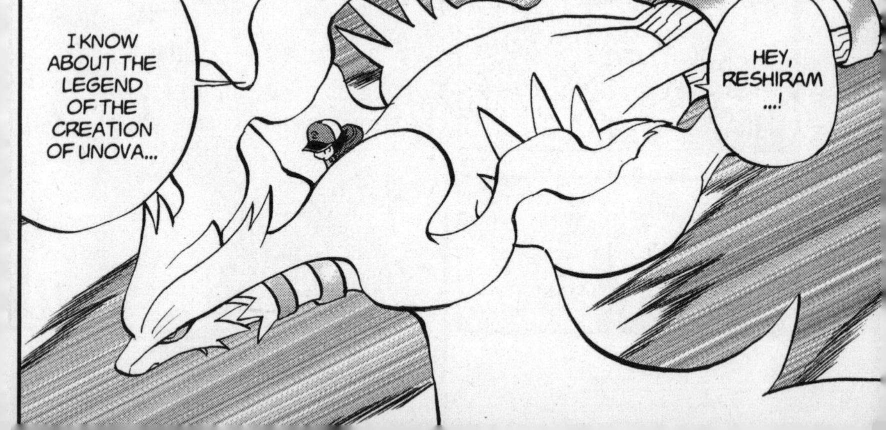
HEY, RESHIRAM ...!
I KNOW ABOUT THE LEGEND OF THE CREATION OF UNOVA...

TWO TWIN PRINCES CREATED UNOVA...
...WITH THE AID OF A POWERFUL DRAGON-TYPE POKÉMON.

BUT EACH OF THE PRINCES WANTED SOMETHING DIFFERENT...
...SO THE LEGENDARY DRAGON-TYPE POKÉMON SPLIT IN TWO...
...AND EACH HALF WENT WITH ONE OF THE PRINCES.

RESHIRAM, YOU...
...WENT WITH THE YOUNGER BROTHER WHO LIVED FOR THE PURSUIT OF "TRUTH"...

SO I'M ONLY THE SECOND PERSON TO RIDE ON YOUR BACK...
hff
hff
DID YOUR FIRST RIDER, THE PRINCE, FEEL OVERWHELMED LIKE ME?
HOW DID HE FIGHT WITH YOU?

...
WHY DID YOU CHOOSE ME ANYWAY...?!
hff
hff

BLACK!
WE'VE COME TO HELP!
WHAT?!
GO, DEINO!
SAMUROTT!
CROAGUNK!
jump

chomp
bonk
tang
krck
Wffff
shattr
ZEKROM'S BODY IS SO TOUGH!

THANKS, BUT...
...I WOULD HAVE BEATEN IT ALREADY IF SIMPLE ATTACKS LIKE THAT WORKED ON ZEKROM.
bounce
snag
OOF!
grab

hff
hff
AND LEARNING MORE ABOUT ITS ATTACKS AND DEFENSES WON'T HELP EITHER...
I NEED TO FIND OUT WHAT'S IN RESHIRAM'S **HEART**.

squeek
fsssssszip
TH-THAT'S ...

DADUNN

AAAAAAARGH!
AAH!
TCH!
Smak
roll
Slip
TING

KRC KRK
OW OW OW!
WHAT WAS THAT FOR, RESHIRAM?!
KRC KRK

BLACK! HAND ME YOUR POKÉDEX!
WHAT?!

AT A TIME LIKE THIS?!
BECAUSE IT'S A TIME LIKE THIS! HURRY!

GO!

WHAT ARE YOU DOING?!
I'M GOING TO UPDATE IT!

LIKE BLACK SAID, I CAN'T HELP HIM DIRECTLY IN BATTLE...
BUT I'M A POKÉMON RESEARCHER! MY KNOWLEDGE AND RESEARCH MIGHT COME IN HANDY SOMEHOW.
63%

I'LL INSTALL ALL THE DATA ON ZEKROM AND RESHIRAM THAT I'VE GATHERED FROM RUINS, DOCUMENTS AND LEGENDS...
klk klk

KNOWING MORE ABOUT THEIR ABILITIES AND CHARACTERIS-TICS MIGHT HELP BLACK FIGURE OUT WHAT'S GO-ING ON INSIDE RESHIRAM'S HEAD...
OKAY! I'M DONE!

THEY'RE BOTH DRAGON-TYPE POKÉMON...
THEY HAVE DRAGON-TYPE BODIES... BUT THEY HAVE ***DIFFERENT*** MOVES!

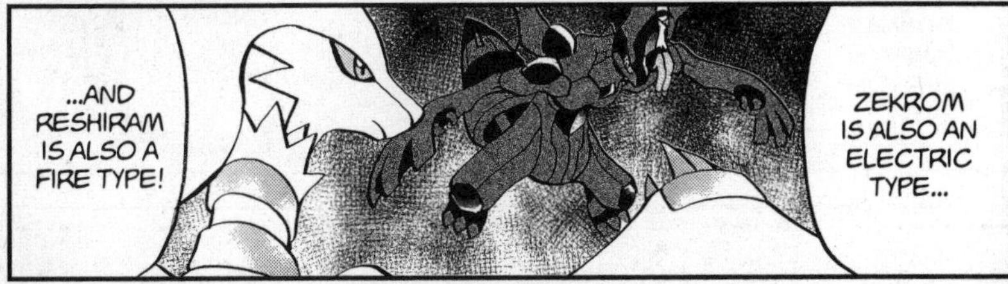
ZEKROM IS ALSO AN ELECTRIC TYPE...
...AND RESHIRAM IS ALSO A FIRE TYPE!

ZEKROM'S TAIL IS SHAPED LIKE AN ELECTRIC GENERATOR.
IT USES IT TO WHIP UP A SURGE OF ELECTRICITY.

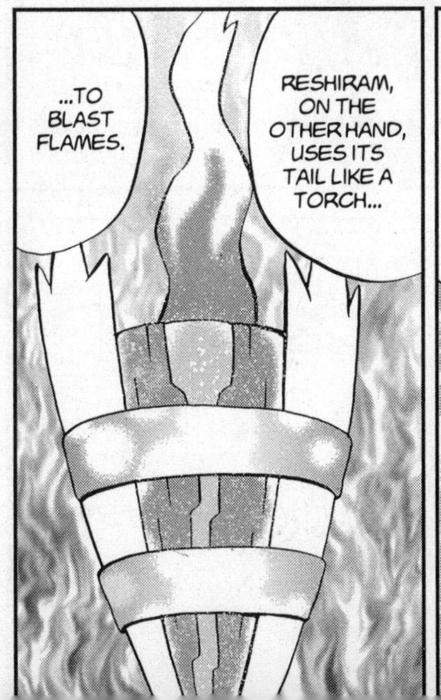
RESHIRAM, ON THE OTHER HAND, USES ITS TAIL LIKE A TORCH...
...TO BLAST FLAMES.

NOW I GET IT...!

...

RESHIRAM'S TAIL STARTED TO SHINE AND BURN AFTER IT GOT HIT BY AN ATTACK. IT MUST HAVE BEEN ANGRY...

I LEARNED THAT FIRST-HAND... ER... FIRST-FOOT!

I BONDED WITH MY POKÉMON DURING BATTLE BY USING MY POKÉDEX TO LEARN MORE ABOUT THEM.
RESHIRAM—THE LIGHT STONE—CHOSE ME...
...BECAUSE I WAS OPPOSED TO TEAM PLASMA AND N'S MISSION.

HA! I GUESS I CAN'T AWAKEN YOU JUST BY SAYING SOMETHING DRAMATIC!

THE WHITE DRAGON-TYPE POKÉMON AND TRUTH OF UNOVA!! SHOW YOURSELF!!
RESHI-RAM
ZEKROM AWOKE FROM ITS STONE FOR N BECAUSE HE HAD AN UNBENDING IDEAL...
I DIDN'T KNOW WHAT MY TRUTH WAS AT FIRST...

RESHIRAM WAS WAITING FOR ME INSIDE THE STONE, WAITING FOR ME TO GET IN TOUCH WITH MY TRUTH!
THERE'S NO NEED FOR ME TO WONDER HOW TO FIGHT THIS BATTLE OR WHY I WAS CHOSEN.

I CAN'T LOSE!
ALL I HAVE TO DO IS FACE ZEKROM WITH THE SAME DEPTH OF FEELING AS YOU, RESHIRAM!

ALL RIGHT!
THIS IS WHERE THE BATTLE REALLY BEGINS, RESHIRAM!

YOU CAN HEAR RESHIRAM'S VOICE?
BLACK...

I SEE...
YOU ARE...
...THE ONE RESHIRAM CHOSE AFTER ALL.

THE HERO...
...OF TRUTH!

SHAAAAAA
ZZZZZPPPP
FZZZZZZZ

ZEK-
ROM HAS
STARTED
TO SPIN ITS
GENERA-
TOR!
IT'S
CREATING
A POWER-
FUL
ELECTRIC
CUR-
RENT...
...AND
ITS TAIL
IS
SHINING
BRIGHT
BLUE!
OVER-
DRIVE!

rmmbl
DADUNNN
FUSION BOLT...
ZEKROM'S SIGNATURE MOVE... WHICH IT CAN USE WHEN IT'S IN AN OVERDRIVE STATE...
hff
hff
IT CREATED A THUNDERCLOUD OUT OF NOWHERE AND SHOT A POWERFUL LIGHTNING BOLT AT US!
hff
hff
RESHI-RAM...

ONE MORE OF THOSE ATTACKS AND WE'RE DONE FOR!

BUT... IT'S THE SAME FOR ZEKROM.
hff
hff

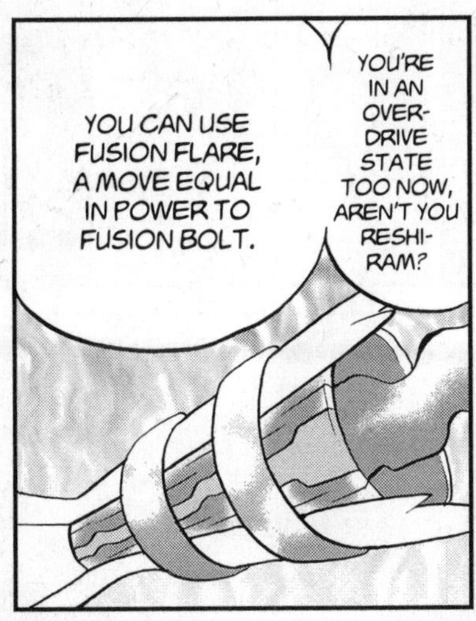
YOU'RE IN AN OVER-DRIVE STATE TOO NOW, AREN'T YOU RESHI-RAM?
YOU CAN USE FUSION FLARE, A MOVE EQUAL IN POWER TO FUSION BOLT.

AND YOU CAN INCREASE THE POWER OF YOUR ATTACK BY USING YOUR MOVE AFTER YOUR OPPONENT USES ***ITS*** MOVE!
hff
hff
hff
BUT N NEVER CALLS OUT HIS ORDERS. HOW WILL I KNOW WHEN ZEKROM'S ABOUT TO STRIKE? WAIT, I HAVE AN IDEA. I WANT YOU TO USE FUSION FLARE WHEN...

rmbl
rmbl
rmbl

rmbl
rmbl

rmbl
rmbl

fffftt
gulp
FOOOSH

Shing
HERE COMES THE AT-TACK... NOW!

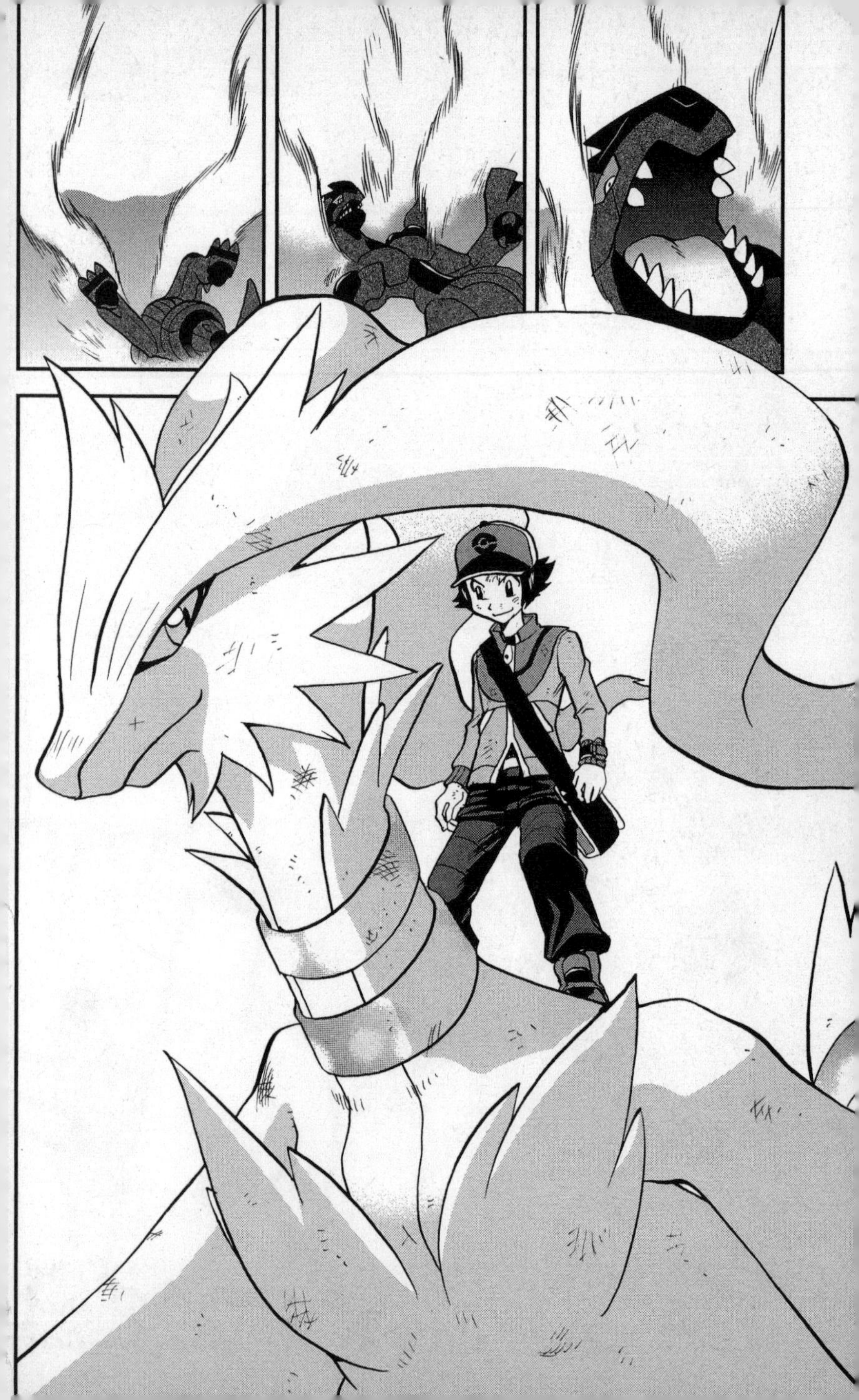

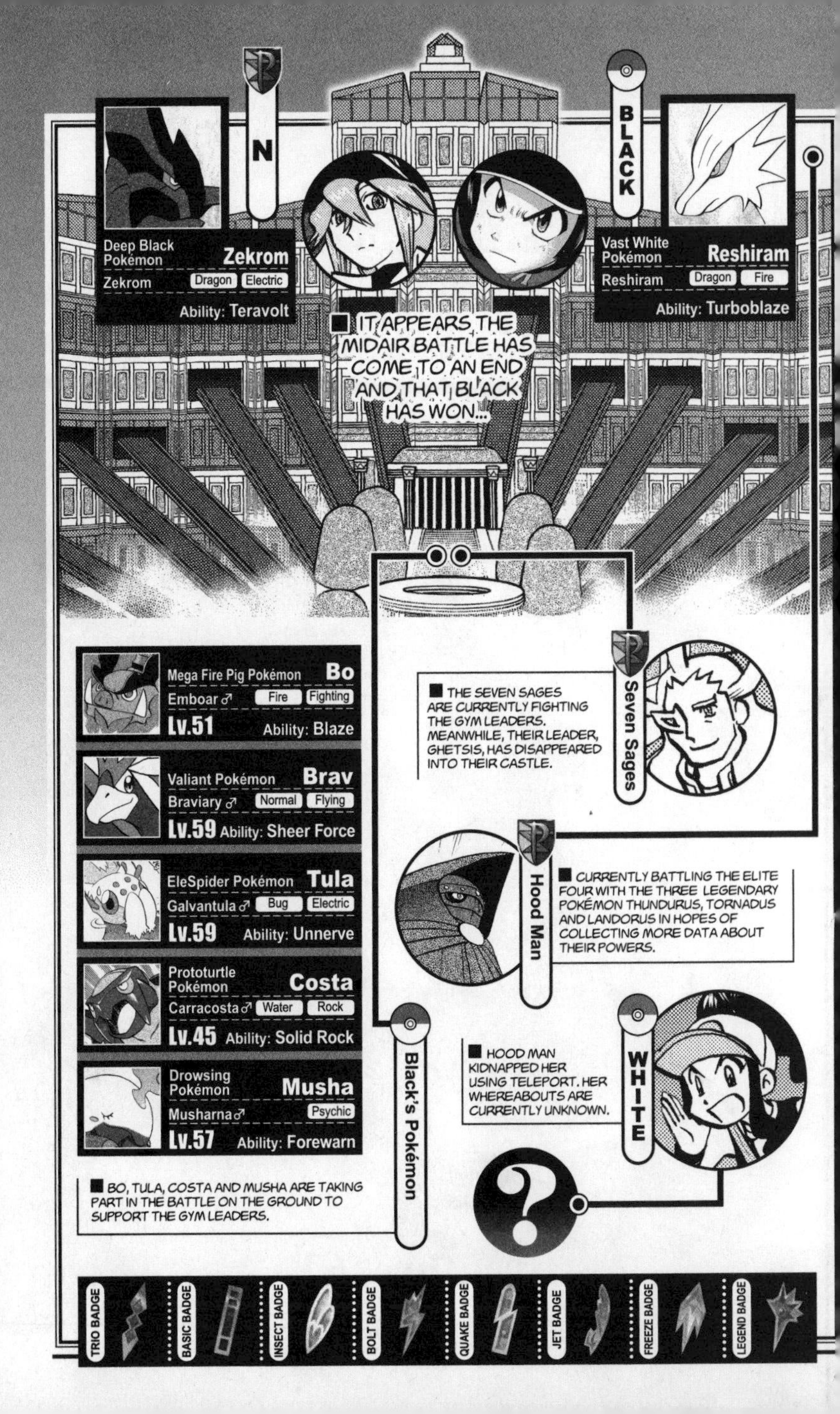
N
Deep Black Pokémon
Zekrom
Zekrom
Dragon
Electric
Ability: Teravolt
BLACK
Vast White Pokémon
Reshiram
Reshiram
Dragon
Fire
Ability: Turboblaze
IT APPEARS THE MIDAIR BATTLE HAS COME TO AN END AND THAT BLACK HAS WON...
Seven Sages
THE SEVEN SAGES ARE CURRENTLY FIGHTING THE GYM LEADERS. MEANWHILE, THEIR LEADER, GHETSIS, HAS DISAPPEARED INTO THEIR CASTLE.
Mega Fire Pig Pokémon
Bo
Emboar ♂
Fire
Fighting
Lv.51
Ability: Blaze
Valiant Pokémon
Brav
Braviary ♂
Normal
Flying
Lv.59
Ability: Sheer Force
EleSpider Pokémon
Tula
Galvantula ♂
Bug
Electric
Lv.59
Ability: Unnerve
Prototurtle Pokémon
Costa
Carracosta ♂
Water
Rock
Lv.45
Ability: Solid Rock
Drowsing Pokémon
Musha
Musharna ♂
Psychic
Lv.57
Ability: Forewarn
Hood Man
CURRENTLY BATTLING THE ELITE FOUR WITH THE THREE LEGENDARY POKÉMON THUNDURUS, TORNADUS AND LANDORUS IN HOPES OF COLLECTING MORE DATA ABOUT THEIR POWERS.
Black's Pokémon
WHITE
HOOD MAN KIDNAPPED HER USING TELEPORT. HER WHEREABOUTS ARE CURRENTLY UNKNOWN.
BO, TULA, COSTA AND MUSHA ARE TAKING PART IN THE BATTLE ON THE GROUND TO SUPPORT THE GYM LEADERS.
TRIO BADGE
BASIC BADGE
INSECT BADGE
BOLT BADGE
QUAKE BADGE
JET BADGE
FREEZE BADGE
LEGEND BADGE

ZEKROM
VS
RESHIRAM
III

Adventure 62
Homecoming

OH!

HE DID IT!
DON'T GET TOO EXCI-TED YET...
AT ANY RATE, HE **DOES** SEEM TO BE RIDING RESHIRAM WITHOUT A PROBLEM NOW...

I'M PROUD TO BE THE ONE WHO OVERSAW HIS TRAINING!
YES!

KRASH
ALL RIGHT! TIME TO WRAP UP THIS BATTLE!

WE'VE ALMOST MADE IT TO THE SECRET LOCATION WHERE THE GYM LEADERS ARE BEING HELD!
YOU CAN DO IT, PATRAT!

THEY'RE TOUGH...
I DON'T UNDER-STAND WHY THESE PEOPLE ARE FIGHTING AGAINST US...

YOU DON'T? IT'S SIMPLE!
Slam

WE ALL WANT...
...TO LIVE TOGETHER WITH POKÉMON.

I TRIED TO EARN THE BADGES I NEEDED TO ENTER THE POKÉMON LEAGUE THIS YEAR...
...BUT I FAILED. AND NOT FOR THE FIRST TIME.

I STILL CAME HERE, THOUGH, BECAUSE I WANTED TO WATCH THE TOURNA-MENT.
AND I LEARNED SOME-THING!

I'M NEVER GOING TO GIVE UP ON MY DREAMS. IF I CAN'T MAKE IT THIS YEAR, I'LL TRY AGAIN NEXT YEAR. AND THE YEAR AFTER THAT. IT'S TAKING ON CHALLENGES AND TRAIN-ING HARD THAT MAKES MY LIFE MEANINGFUL—NOT JUST WINNING.
I NEED GYM LEADERS TO TRAIN WITH, AND THE POKÉMON LEAGUE TO SET AN EXAMPLE OF EXCELLENCE.

AND THAT'S MY POKÉMON'S DREAM TOO.
THEY DON'T NEED YOUR SO-CALLED POKÉMON LIBERATION!

THE SAME GOES FOR ME!
OUR POKÉMON ...
...*CHOOSE* TO LIVE WITH UNSKILLED TRAINERS LIKE US OF THEIR OWN FREE WILL!

WE'RE ALL GROWNUPS WHO GAVE UP OUR DREAMS...
BUT OUR POKÉMON HELPED US GET OUR DREAMS BACK... AFTER MEETING THAT BOY.
WE'RE ALL HERE TO WATCH THE BOY WHO HELPED US FULFILL HIS OWN DREAM HERE TODAY.

SO WE CAN'T LET YOU GO ON MANIPULATING PEOPLE INTO GIVING UP THEIR POKÉMON AND LEAVING THEM TO FEND FOR THEMSELVES IN THE WILD.
DNK
DNK
DNK
YOU WON'T DE-FEAT US!
DNK
DNK

OKAY, SHOKO!
LET'S DO IT, PRINCESS!

AFTER YOU!
ZZZOOP

FLAME BURST!
FWOOOS

NOW!
zip zip zip
nibbl
nibbl
nibbl
snap
HUH?!
tnk

WHAT?!
I HAD NO IDEA SUCH UNENLIGHTENED COMMONERS WERE CAPABLE OF SUCH A THING!

"UNENLIGHTENED"...? HEY!
WHAT DOES HE MEAN BY "UNENLIGHTENED"?!
THEY BADLY UNDERESTIMATED US.
LOOKS LIKE YOU'RE BEGINNING TO SHOW YOUR TRUE COLORS!
THEY SURE ARE, LENORA!

WHATEVER!
I'VE BEEN GOING STIR CRAZY IN CAPTIVITY ALL THIS TIME!
IT'S TIME TO RUMBLE!
DRILL RUN!
kerash

STRUGGLE BUG!
WILD CHARGE!
HURRI-CANE!

ting
WOOOSH

whoosh
WAIT!
WHOA!
OOF!
smak
URGH...!
skreeech

OWW... MARSHAL ?!
WHAT ARE YOU DOING, BLACK ?!
THAT'S *MY* LINE!

THUNDURUS, TORNADUS AND LANDORUS DISAPPEARED WHILE WE WERE FIGHTING. WE'RE TRYING TO FIND THEM.

DID YOUR MUNNA—MUSHARNA—RETURN TO YOU?
HUH...?

WE NOTICED IT FLOATING AROUND THE STADIUM WHEN WE WERE GETTING READY FOR THE ELITE FOUR BATTLES.
I COULD TELL RIGHT AWAY THAT IT WAS YOUR MUNNA. IT SEEMED NERVOUS ABOUT SEEING YOU AGAIN, BUT I TOLD IT NOT TO WORRY AND TO GO FIND YOU AS SOON AS IT COULD.

THE REASON IT LEFT YOU BEFORE WAS...
...BECAUSE IT WANTED TO FIND AN ENERGY SOURCE. TO BE EXACT, IT WANTED TO EVOLVE VERY BADLY.

I GAVE IT A MOON STONE TO HELP IT ALONG.

SO *THAT'S* WHY... IT WASN'T BECAUSE OF ME.

ALSO ...
...N AND ZEKROM HAVE GONE INTO THAT CASTLE.

FOL-LOW THEM IN THERE!

HUNNHH ...?
WHERE... AM I...?
OH GOOD!
YOU'VE FINALLY WOKEN UP!

I'M CON-CORDIA.
I'M ANTHEA.
AND THIS IS N'S ROOM.

N'S ROOM ?!
BOM
WAIT! WE WON'T HURT YOU.
HOOD MAN BROUGHT YOU HERE.
WHY ?
WE DON'T KNOW. WE HAVE NO IDEA WHAT GOES ON IN HIS MIND.
MAY-BE ...

N RELEASED ALL THE POKÉMON HE LIVED WITH BEFORE HIS FINAL BATTLE.
TYMPOLE, GURDURR, ARCHEOPS, DARMAN-ITAN, ZORUA– AND THAT TEPIG AS WELL.
BUT THE TEPIG...
...CAME ***BACK***.
GIGI!

YOU SAID THIS WAS N'S ROOM...
WHAT ARE YOU DOING HERE?
OH, WE TAKE CARE OF N.
WHAT ?!

N GREW UP IN THE COMPANY OF POKÉMON WHO WERE MISTREATED BY HUMANS...
...ALL BY HIMSELF IN THIS VERY ROOM.

SINCE HE WAS A SMALL CHILD, N HAS HAD THE SPECIAL ABILITY TO HEAR THE VOICES OF POKÉMON.
HE HAD NO FAMILY AND PEOPLE THOUGHT HE WAS CRAZY...

SO GHETSIS ...
...TOOK N IN.

GHETSIS ADOPT-ED...
...N AS HIS SON.

THEN GHETSIS MADE SURE N ONLY HEARD...
...THE VOICES OF ABUSED POKÉMON YEAR AFTER YEAR.

WHEN N LET HIS POKÉMON GO FREE, HE TOLD THIS TEPIG...

WHETHER YOU KEEP FIGHTING POKÉMON BATTLES OR GO BACK TO PERFORMING IN SHOW BUSINESS...
...IS UP TO YOU.

ALL OF YOU...
I WANT YOU TO KNOW THAT...

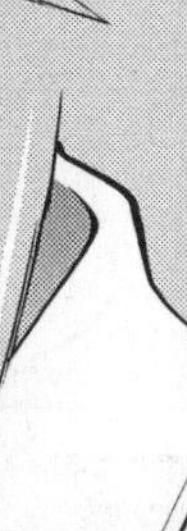
...IF YOU MEET A PERSON YOU REALLY LIKE...
...THERE'S NOTHING WRONG WITH STAYING WITH THEM.

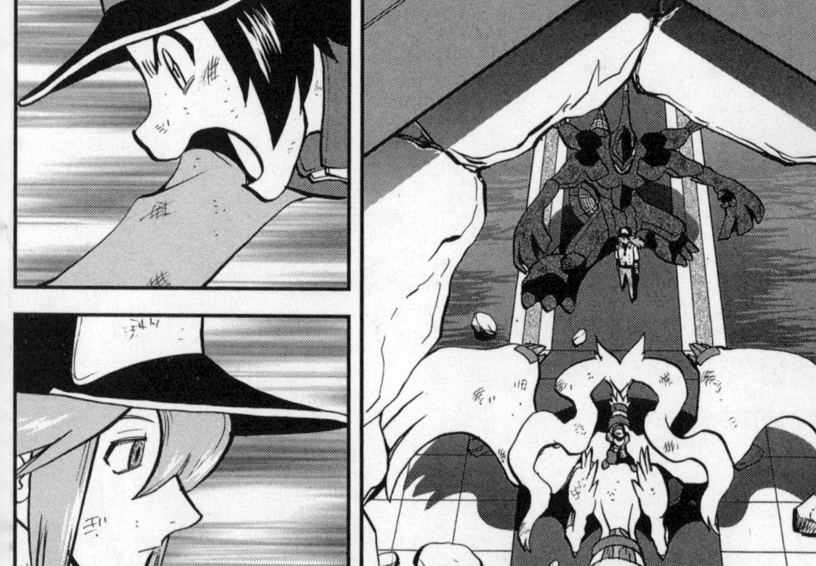

"IF YOU MEET A PERSON YOU REALLY LIKE...
"...THERE'S NOTHING WRONG WITH STAYING WITH THEM"...

N...
...SAID THAT? REALLY?

AFTER BEING REJECTED BY SO MANY PEOPLE AND GHETSIS'S BRAINWASHING, N TRULY BELIEVED IT WAS HIS RESPONSIBILITY TO LIBERATE POKÉMON.

GHETSIS THOUGHT N WAS SO FOCUSED ON THIS IDEAL OF POKÉMON LIBERATION THAT HE WOULDN'T BE INFLUENCED BY THE OUTSIDE WORLD.
SO AFTER HIS CORONATION, GHETSIS ALLOWED N TO GO OUT AND PROSELYTIZE AS THE KING OF TEAM PLASMA.

BUT THAT'S WHEN...
...N DISCOVERED THE TRUTH...

I WAS ABLE TO HEAR YOUR TEPIG'S VOICE.
I NEVER IMAGINED A POKÉMON MIGHT FEEL THAT WAY...
I'VE COME ACROSS YET ANOTHER...
PUZZLE I CANNOT SOLVE.

AN UNSOLVABLE PUZZLE...
ACTUALLY, THIS PUZZLE WAS SIMPLE TO DECIPHER.
BUT N DIDN'T LIKE THE ANSWER, SO AT FIRST HE REFUSED TO ACCEPT IT.
IT WAS A PUZZLE HE DIDN'T *WANT* TO SOLVE—BECAUSE IT CONTRADICTED EVERYTHING HE'D BEEN TAUGHT AND BELIEVED IN UP TILL THAT POINT.

THIS PERSON REALLY GETS ME.
I WANT TO BE WITH HIM FOREVER, TO SHARE MY LIFE WITH HIM.

rmblrm
bl
rmbl
rmbl
rmbl

HEY! WHERE ARE THE SEVEN SAGES?!
HUH?

THEY'RE **GONE**!
GRRR! THEY MUST HAVE ESCAPED BY HIDING AMONGST THOSE TEAM PLASMA GRUNTS...

murmur
murmur

tmp
tmp
tmp

dash
eeuurk
SHIFT GEAR!

ZOOP
ZOOP
GEAR GRIND!
ZOOP

urrrk
NOW, BI-SHARP!
jmp
jmp
um mrk

smak

TURNS OUT YOU'RE NOT LIKE THEY SAY YOU ARE, GRIMSLEY ...
I HEARD YOU ONLY CARE ABOUT YOURSELF.
BUT IT LOOKS LIKE YOU CARE ABOUT OTHERS AFTER ALL.

WHAT THEY SAY IS TRUE. I'M ONLY DOING THIS FOR ME. BECAUSE I CAN'T STAND IT ANYMORE...
WHAT DO YOU MEAN ...?

WELL, FOR THE PAST FEW MONTHS, MY TABLE'S BEEN SHAKING...

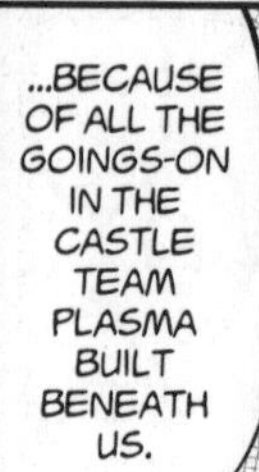
...BECAUSE OF ALL THE GOINGS-ON IN THE CASTLE TEAM PLASMA BUILT BENEATH US.

IT'S RUINING MY CARD AND ROULETTE GAMES!! HOW ARE WE SUPPOSED TO PLAY ON AN UNSTEADY SURFACE?!
SO THERE YOU HAVE IT...

NOW LET'S SEE WHAT'S UNDER THAT HEAVY HOOD OF YOURS!
WFFF

BOM

ZZ
WZZ

WHAT SPEED! INCREDIBLE!
IT DIDN'T USE TELEPORT... IT WAS JUST INCREDIBLY FAST!

WHO... **WAS** THAT?

IT WAS RIDING A KLINKLANG UNTIL A MOMENT AGO, BUT JUST NOW IT...

fwip
fwip
fwip

OH MY!
HOW ADORABLE!
OH!
I SEE YOU STILL WANT TO BE A PERFORMER!
tmp

BUT YOU'RE N'S POKÉMON NOW.
SO I'LL WRITE UP A CONTRACT FOR YOU TO PERFORM WITH BW AGENCY. DOES THAT WORK FOR YOU?

nod

GOOD! NOW LET'S GO FIND BLACK AND N!

SMAK

NUTS!
IT STILL HAS THE STRENGTH TO KEEP ON FIGHTING!

IF ONLY I COULD HIT IT ONE MORE TIME...!

TWO ZEK-ROMS ?!

WHAT THE...?

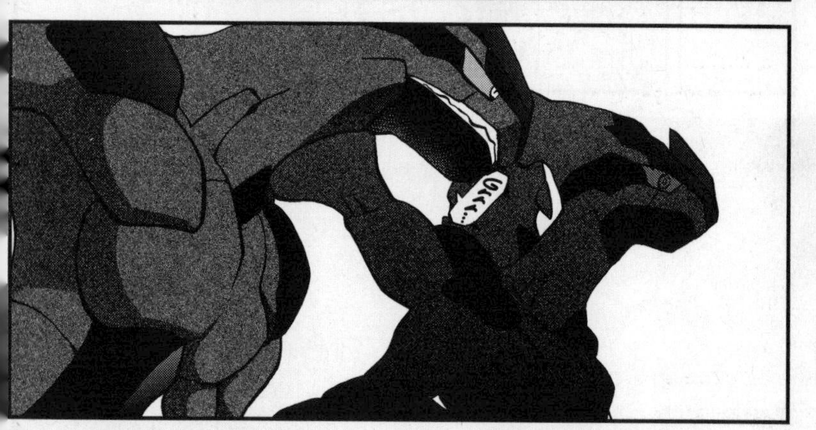
Grrr...

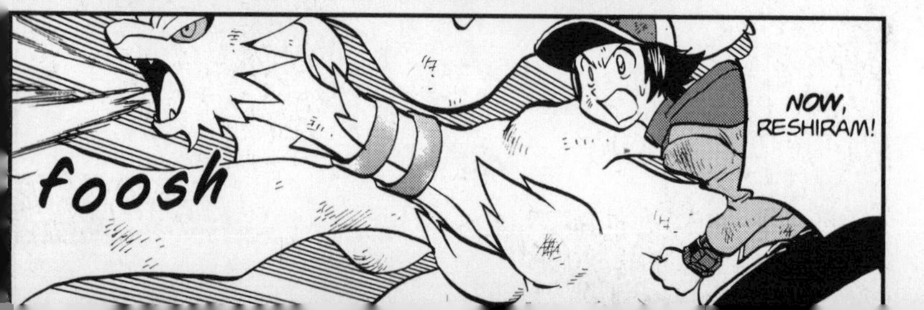
NOW, RESHIRAM!
foosh

WUM
WUM
WUM
WUM
WUM
DRAGON PULSE!

fwump

WHY...?

I DON'T UNDER-STAND ...

thnk
ZOOP ZOOP ZOOP

ZORUA ...

WHY ARE YOU HERE?
I SET YOU FREE! WHY DID YOU COME BACK?

ISN'T IT OBVIOUS ...?

ZORUA WANTS TO HELP YOU.
DON'T YOU GET IT?

YES... I DO NOW...

ZORUA WANTS TO *BE* WITH ME.
THAT'S WHY IT CAME BACK...
YOU AND GIGI BOTH...

BUT YOU SHOULDN'T HAVE TRANS-FORMED INTO ZEK-ROM!
THAT WAS NAUGH-TY!
lift

ZEKROM
VS
RESHIRAM
IV

Adventure 63
The Power of Dreams

I FOUND THEM!
THERE THEY ARE!
I GUESS THAT STORY ABOUT THEM BEING ABLE TO FLY AT 200 MILES PER HOUR IS TRUE, HUH?
WE KEEP LOSING THEM IN THE CLOUDS!
WE ARE THE ***ELITE FOUR***!
PLAYING TAG IS UNDIGNIFIED.

I'LL TAKE CARE OF LAND-ORUS!
I'LL SUPPORT YOU WITH TELEKINESIS!

WHAT'S HE DOING?

WONDERFUL! ABSOLUTELY WONDERFUL!
THE THREE LEGENDARY POKÉMON'S EMOTIONS HAVE BEEN HEIGHTENED BY THE FIERCE ATTACKS FROM THE ELITE FOUR!

THAT SHOULD DRAW OUT THEIR **HIDDEN POWER**! AHA HA HA...!

AND NOW THAT THEY'RE PROVOKED...

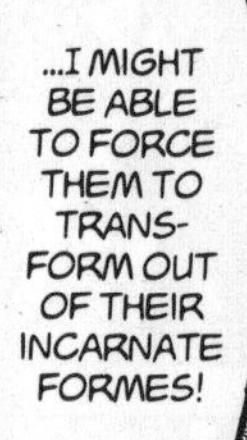
...I MIGHT BE ABLE TO FORCE THEM TO TRANSFORM OUT OF THEIR INCARNATE FORMES!

I'LL GIVE IT A TRY...
rstl

?

hff
hff

IS HE ASLEEP?
OH.

HE HASN'T SAID A THING FOR QUITE A WHILE NOW...

MUST BE NICE TO BE ABLE TO RELAX...
...NOW THAT EVERY-THING'S SETTLED.

HEY...
IS THE BATTLE OVER?

YOU KNOW WHAT, MU-SHA?
I HAD NO IDEA YOU'D FLOWN OFF TO TRAIN ON YOUR OWN.

I HEARD YOU WERE WORRIED BECAUSE MY DREAM HAD CHANGED...
YOU WORKED REALLY HARD TO EVOLVE, DIDN'T YOU...?

HEH... WE NEED EACH OTHER, DON'T WE?

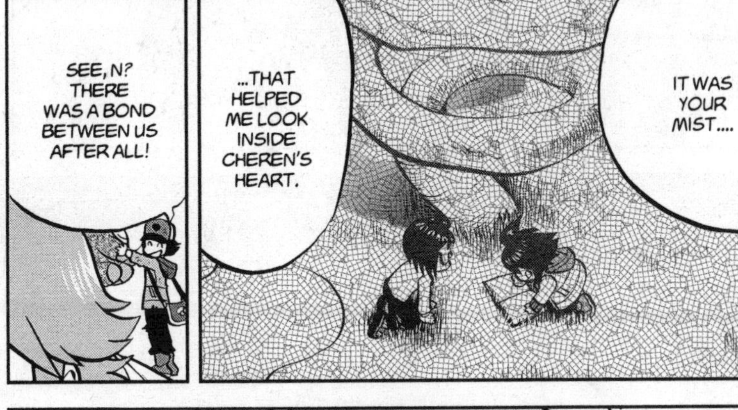
IT WAS YOUR MIST....
...THAT HELPED ME LOOK INSIDE CHEREN'S HEART.
SEE, N? THERE WAS A BOND BETWEEN US AFTER ALL!

BUT I GUESS I DON'T NEED TO TELL HIM THAT.
HE CAN SENSE THE FEELINGS OF POKÉMON.

WHY ARE YOU HERE?

PITIFUL...
ABSOLUTELY PITIFUL. AND YOU CALL YOURSELF A MEMBER OF THE HARMONIA FAMILY?

GHETSIS! YOU...
WHAT DO YOU MEAN BY "FAMILY" ?!

EXACTLY WHAT IT SOUNDS LIKE.
THAT PITIFUL YOUNG MAN ON THE FLOOR THERE IS MY ADOPTED SON...
...NATURAL HARMONIA GROPIUS.

SO GHETSIS, THE LEADER OF THE SEVEN SAGES OF TEAM PLASMA...
...IS N'S FATHER ?!

I SEE NO REASON TO KEEP YOU IN THE DARK ANY LONGER.
I HAD N PURSUE A SINGULAR IDEAL SO HE COULD TURN THE DARK STONE BACK INTO THE LEGENDARY POKÉMON ZEKROM...

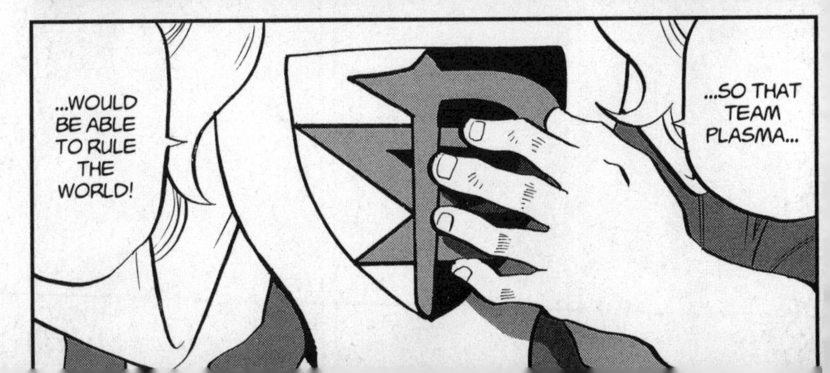
...SO THAT TEAM PLASMA...
...WOULD BE ABLE TO RULE THE WORLD!

THAT IS MY—
AND TEAM
PLASMA'S—
IDEAL...
THE
LIBERATION OF
OTHER
PEOPLE'S
POKÉMON...

RULE
THE...
WORLD
?!

BUT AT FIRST
WE COULDN'T
CONVINCE
PEOPLE TO
ACCEPT IT
OR DO AS WE
SAID.
HOWEVER,
COMMON
MINDS ARE
EASILY
INFLUENCED BY
AUTHORITY AND
POWER...

THAT IS
WHY WE
NEEDED
A KING...
...A
HERO...
...AND A
LEGEND-
ARY
POKÉ-
MON.

WELL
DONE...

...SON.

ZEKROM
RE-
SPONDED
TO YOUR
IDEAL...
...AND
RETURNED
TO THE
STATE OF
THE BLACK
DRAGON-
TYPE
POKÉMON.

THE CHAMPION, ALDER, WAS DEFEATED. THE GYM LEADERS WERE CAPTURED. WE TOOK OVER THE POKÉMON LEAGUE STADIUM.
AND ALL OF UNOVA WITNESSED HOW POWERLESS THEY WERE IN COMPARISON TO TEAM PLASMA.

CONSEQUENTLY, THEY DECIDED THERE MUST BE SOMETHING TO OUR MESSAGE! BECAUSE IGNORANT PEOPLE THINK "MIGHT IS RIGHT." AND NOW THEY ARE READY AND WILLING TO BEND TO OUR AUTHORITY AND FOLLOW OUR EVERY COMMAND!
WE KNEW WE COULD MANIPULATE PEOPLE INTO FOLLOWING TEAM PLASMA AND ACCEPTING OUR SUPPOSED IDEAL.

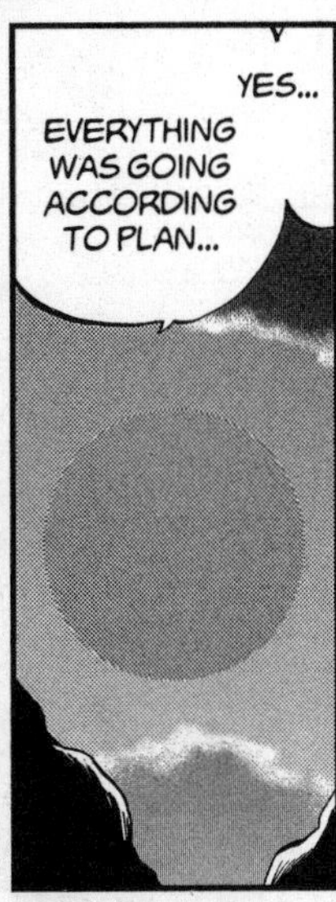
YES...
EVERYTHING WAS GOING ACCORDING TO PLAN...

... UNTIL ...
...MY FOOL OF A SON...

...DECIDED TO BATTLE THE HERO OF TRUTH AND RESHIRAM.
IT WAS AS IF HE WANTED TO PROVE HE WAS REALLY A HERO!

AND TO TOP IT OFF...
...N **LOST**!

BUT I WON'T LET MY MASTER PLAN BE THWARTED...
ALL I NEED TO DO TO PROCEED IS TO GET RID OF THIS ... ***INCONVENIENT TRUTH.***

WHAT DO YOU MEAN?!

ISN'T IT OBVIOUS? I'M GOING TO GET RID OF ***YOU.***
HYDREIGON... BURN HIM TO A CRISP.
KAFWOOSH

ARGH!
YOU CAN'T DEFEAT ME THAT EASILY!

YOU THINK NOT? HA! RESHIRAM DOESN'T HAVE THE STRENGTH TO FIGHT ANYMORE!
TRUE, BUT... RESHIRAM ISN'T MY ONLY POKÉMON!

COSTA, EXTIN-GUISH THAT FIRE!
BO, CRUSH HYDREIGON!
yoink
WHOA!!

ZZZT ZZZT ZZZT ZZZ
SPLOOP

OF COURSE NOT.
HE'S NOTHING BUT A FRONT.

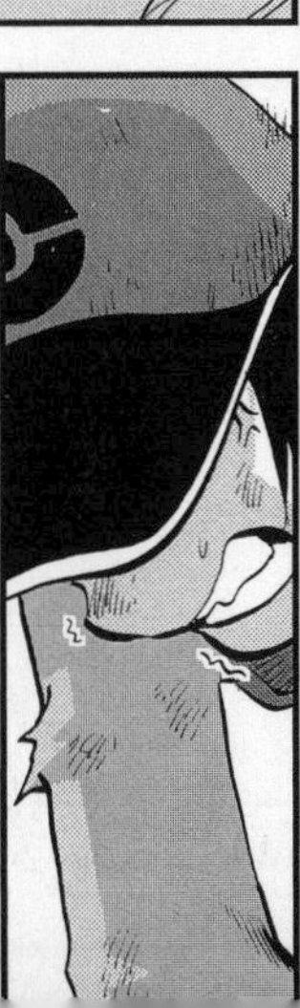

N... YOU DIDN'T HEAR ALL THIS, DID YOU? YOU'RE STILL OUT COLD, RIGHT?

I REALLY HOPE YOU DIDN'T HEAR HOW YOUR FATHER TRICKED YOU...
HOW HE *USED* YOU...

GHETSIS!

I'M REALLY ...
...REALLY REALLY REALLY GONNA BEAT YOU NOW!
BUT HOW?! THINK! THINK!

BRAV, I NEED YOU TO BREAK FREE SOMEHOW!

EELEKTROSS IS FIGHTING TWO OF MY POKÉMON... THAT'S THE ONLY CHANCE I'VE GOT!

Krc Klll

flap

KAZZZ
IZZ
Smash

KRASH

I CAN'T LOSE! IF I LOSE NOW...
...HE'LL TRICK THE PEOPLE OF UNOVA!

KLUMP

JUST LIKE HE TRICKED N!

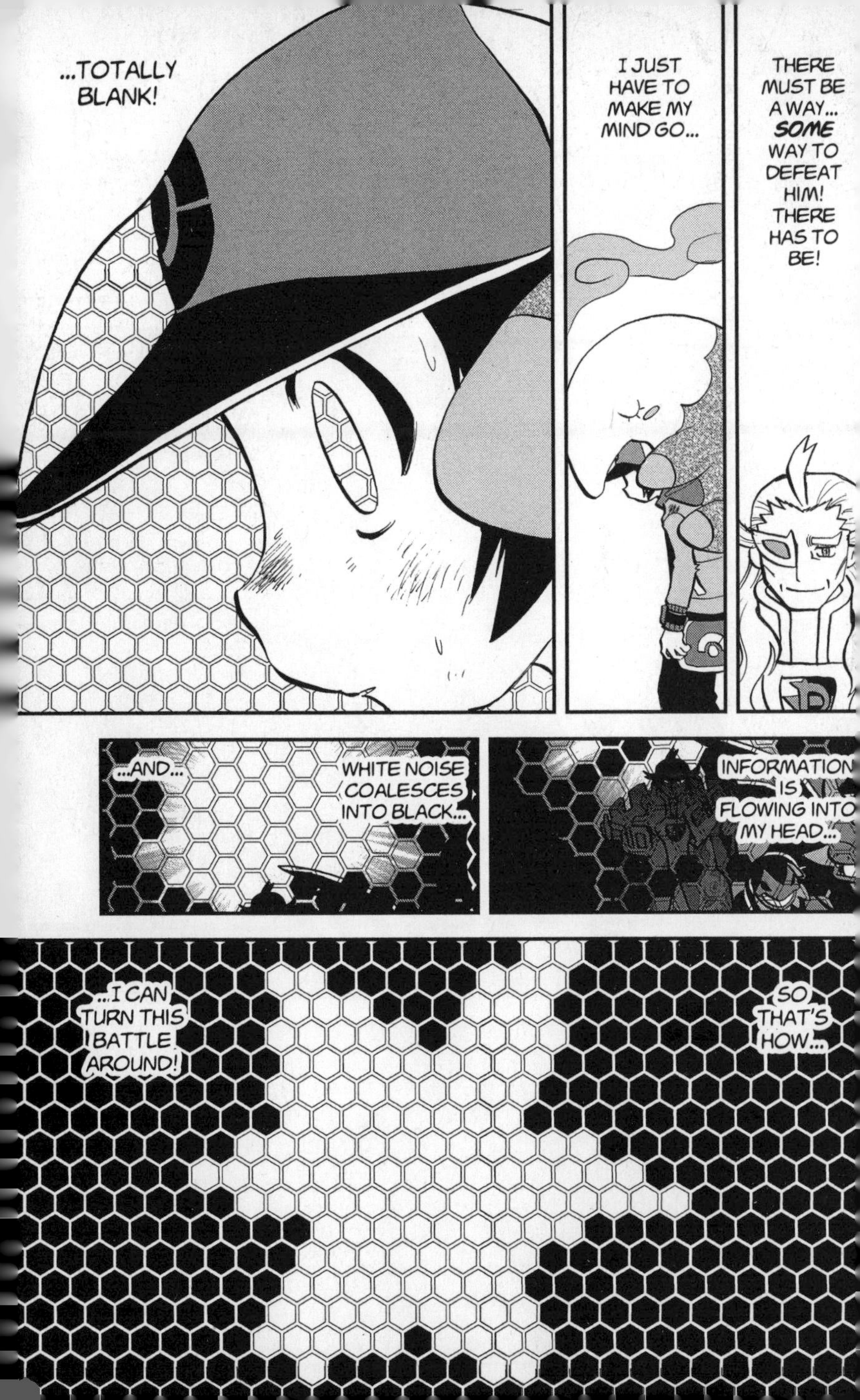
THERE MUST BE A WAY... *SOME* WAY TO DEFEAT HIM! THERE HAS TO BE!
I JUST HAVE TO MAKE MY MIND GO...
...TOTALLY BLANK!
INFORMATION IS FLOWING INTO MY HEAD...
WHITE NOISE COALESCES INTO BLACK...
...AND...
SO THAT'S HOW...
...I CAN TURN THIS BATTLE AROUND!

MUSHA! THE SUN!
SHOOT THE SUN!

pa chew

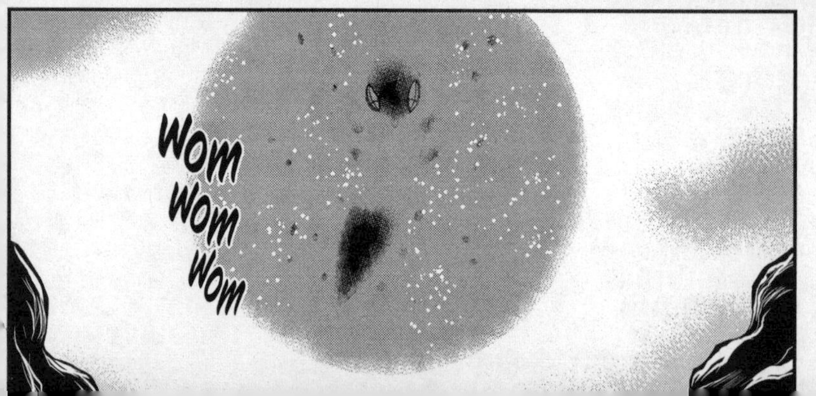
wom wom wom

KIK
THERE WAS ANOTHER POKÉMON HIDING IN THE SETTING SUN...!

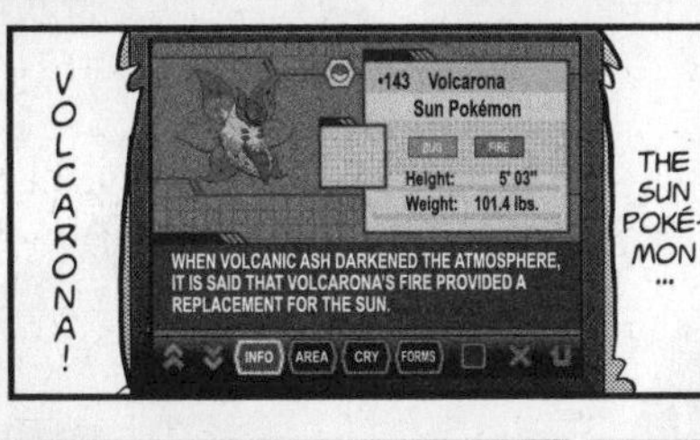
THE SUN POKÉMON...
VOLCARONA!
•143 Volcarona
Sun Pokémon
Height: 5' 03"
Weight: 101.4 lbs.
WHEN VOLCANIC ASH DARKENED THE ATMOSPHERE, IT IS SAID THAT VOLCARONA'S FIRE PROVIDED A REPLACEMENT FOR THE SUN.
INFO
AREA
CRY
FORMS

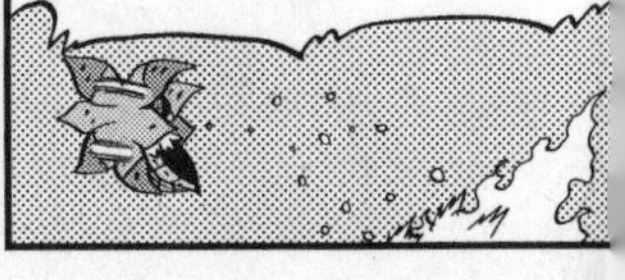
THIS ISN'T HYDREIGON'S FIRE AFTER ALL... THE EMBER SCALES FROM VOLCARONA'S WINGS ARE CATCHING FIRE THE MOMENT THEY FALL TO THE GROUND.

THAT'S WHY THESE FLAMES KEEP FOLLOWING US WHEREVER WE GO. SO, BRAV...

...USE WHIRLWIND TO BLAST THE BURNING SCALES AWAY!
WSSSHHH

VOLCARONA IS A BUG- AND FIRE-TYPE POKÉMON!
COSTA, STONE EDGE!

THK
THK

MUSHA, HIDDEN POWER!
BRAV...
...SKY DROP!
TULA, X-SCISSOR!
BO, FLARE BLITZ!

THK
THK

VOLCARONA...! HOW COULD VOLCARONA BE SO EASILY DEFEATED?!

AND I EVEN HANDED A LARVESTA TO ONE OF THE SHADOW TRIAD WHEN I FOUND ITS EGG AT RELIC CASTLE!
LEGEND HAS IT THAT VOLCARONA REPLACED THE SUN WHEN VOLCANIC ASHES DARKENED THE ATMOSPHERE...

KWATHUD
YOU'RE NOT GOING ANY-WHERE, GHETSIS!
STONE EDGE!
tnk tnk tnk

THIS IS WHERE YOUR TEAM PLASMA IDEAL...
...COMES TO AN END!

I CAN SEE THEM IN THE MIRROR ...

BUT...

...THEY WON'T *TRANS-FORM*!

I KNOW THAT...
...A MIRROR IS THE KEY.
BUT MAYBE NOT *THIS* MIRROR...?

OH...

IT LOOKS LIKE GHETSIS HAS BEEN DEFEATED.

TIME TO CALL IT QUITS THEN!
SCHLOOP
BESIDES, I HAVE A MIRROR TO FIND.

WAIT!

SORRY, CAN'T STAY!
HOW-EVER, THIS HAS BEEN MOST ENJOY-ABLE.
I'M SURE WE'LL MEET AGAIN SOMEDAY. TILL THEN!

WZZZZZZZZZ

BLACK ...

NOW WHAT SHOULD I DO WITH GHETSIS?
JUST HAND HIM OVER TO DRAYDEN?

BOSS!

ZEKROM
VS
RESHIRAM
V

Adventure 64
A Difficult Parting

LET'S GO DOWN!

THE ONES WE REALLY NEED TO FREE...
...ARE THOSE WHO'VE BEEN BOUND BY TEAM PLASMA'S ABUSE OF THE WORDS "FREEDOM" AND "LIBERA-TION"...

COULD YOU...
...WAIT A MOMENT?

N...

YOU'RE WITH THEM TOO, GIGI?

YES. THE HOOD MAN PUT ME IN YOUR ROOM.
THAT'S WHERE WE WERE REUNIT-ED.

I SEE...
AND YOU WERE ABLE TO LEARN WHAT GIGI WANTS?

YES.
AFTER EXPERIENCING POKÉMON BATTLES, GIGI MADE HER CHOICE.

AND I HAVE *YOU* TO THANK FOR THAT...
...N.
YOU HELPED ME HEAR GIGI'S VOICE.

...

I NEVER WOULD HAVE THOUGHT WE COULD HAVE A RELAXED CONVERSATION LIKE THIS...
IT'S STRANGE...

MAYBE...
...THIS IS WHAT I'VE BEEN LONGING FOR ALL ALONG...

N...

WORKS FOR ME!
I'M GLAD WE CAN TALK TO EACH OTHER LIKE THIS NOW!
LOOKS LIKE ALL'S WELL THAT ENDS WELL!

THE FIRST TIME I BATTLED WITH YOU IN ACCUMULA TOWN, MUSHA ATE YOUR DREAM AND PUFFED IT OUT THROUGH ITS MIST...

INSIDE THE MIST, I COULD SEE...
...YOUR GENTLE AND PEACE-FUL...
... DREAM.

IT'S PROBABLY BECAUSE I SAW YOUR DREAM THAT...

...EVEN THOUGH AT FIRST I FELT I COULD NEVER FORGIVE YOU... SOMEWHERE IN MY HEART...

...I KNEW... YOU WERE A GOOD GUY.
A REALLY GOOD GUY WHO ALWAYS ONLY WANTED THE BEST FOR POKÉMON.
THAT WAS ONE TRUTH I WAS SURE OF.

...

I BEGAN HAVING DOUBTS WHEN I FOUGHT YOU IN ACCUMULA TOWN...

THAT DOUBT CONTINUED TO GROW THE MORE I TRAVELED AROUND UNOVA.

I FOUGHT YOU TO TEST MY RESOLVE... TO CHANNEL MY IDEAL INTO ZEKROM TO SEE HOW RIGHTEOUS IT WAS.

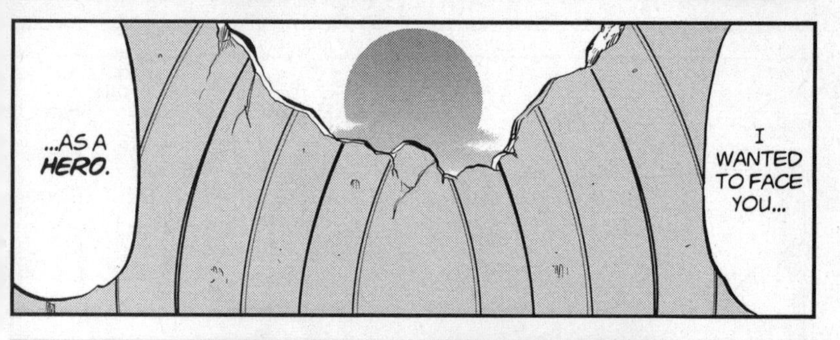
I WANTED TO FACE YOU...
...AS A ***HERO***.

BUT... ALTHOUGH I CAN HEAR POKÉMON'S VOICES... I NEVER TRULY...
...UNDERSTOOD THEM LIKE YOU DO. I WAS NEVER A MATCH FOR YOU TO BEGIN WITH.

FORGIVE ME, BLACK.

NOW I NEED TO GO AND FIGURE OUT...
...WHAT'S NEXT.

GOODBYE.

FWAPP

N!

raaooorr

RESHI-RAM IS ROAR-ING SO LOUDLY!
YOU'RE RIGHT...

IT MUST FEEL LIKE...
...IT'S LOST HALF OF ITS SOUL...

drag
?!
drag drag
WHAT THE ...?!
WE'RE BEING PULLED OVER TO RESHI-RAM!

STAND BACK, BOSS!
THIS FEELS A LOT LIKE THE TIME RESHIRAM WAS AWAKENED FROM THE LIGHT STONE...

EVERYTHING THAT GOT RELEASED IN THAT MOMENT...
...IS BEING SUCKED BACK INSIDE!!

I GUESS RESHIRAM IS GOING TO TURN BACK INTO THE STONE NOW THAT IT'S FINISHED ITS BATTLE AGAINST ZEKROM!
WE NEED TO BACK UP—AND FAST!

SPLEN-DID.
YOU TOO WILL GET DRAGGED IN AND TURNED TO STONE.

BLACK!
DON'T WORRY, BOSS!

HEY, GHET-SIS!
YOU'RE FRUS-TRATED, AREN'T YOU? BE-CAUSE YOU CAN'T DO ANY-THING TO ME!

FRUS-TRAT-ED ...?
ON THE CON-TRARY. I AM ECSTAT-IC.

THE HERO WHO ONCE STOOD IN MY WAY IS PROVIDING ME WITH THE PERFECT MEANS TO RID MYSELF OF HIM.

YANK!

tmp
BLACK!
GH...

GHET-SIS!
HOW DID YOU GET OUT ...?!

I HAVE FRIENDS.

THIS IS TRULY GRATI-FYING...

squeeeeee
AND THIS WILL BE THE LAST TIME WE SHALL EVER MEET...
...HERO OF TRUTH.

WOOMFF

BLACK!
STAY BACK! DON'T COME NEAR ME!

OR YOU'LL GET DRAGGED IN AS WELL...!

HOLD ON! I'LL GET HELP!
BOSS !!

I HAVEN'T ...
...BROKEN MY PROMISE, YOU KNOW!

WHAT ARE YOU TALKING ABOUT ?!

YOU'VE FORGOT-TEN ...?
REMEM-BER WHAT YOU SAID IN CAS-TELIA CITY?

IF I EVER MADE IT INTO THE POKÉMON LEAGUE...
ZIP
...I SHOULD WEAR *THIS*!

Pokémon
BW
Agency

OUR COMPANY LOGO...

...YOU'LL WEAR OUR COMPANY LOGO!
I'M GOING TO ENTER THE POKEMON LEAGUE! AND...
...I'LL BE WEARING YOUR COMPANY LOGO ON MY UNIFORM, JUST LIKE I PROMISED!

YOU REMEMBERED...
OF COURSE I REMEMBERED!
I DID SOME RESEARCH AND FIGURED OUT THAT THE BEST TIME TO PUT IT ON WOULD BE...
...AFTER WINNING THE TOURNAMENT THAT EARNS ME THE RIGHT TO FACE THE ELITE FOUR.
THAT'S WHEN I'D BE SURROUNDED BY THE MEDIA.

I WAS GOING TO WHIP OFF MY JACKET AND SHOUT...
..."FOR TV DRAMAS, MOVIES, COMMERCIALS, STAGE SHOWS AND PRINT ADS...
"...YOU CAN ALWAYS COUNT ON BW AGENCY!"

BUT I MESSED UP.

DID I WORK HARD ENOUGH...
...TO PAY YOU BACK FOR THE EQUIPMENT I DAMAGED?
DID I...?
BOS...

YOU...
...DON'T HAVE TO WORRY ABOUT PAYING ME BACK ANY-MORE...
AFTER ALL...
...YOU ...
WAIT! DON'T GO!

BLACK!!

AND IT'S ALL THANKS TO YOU, GHETSIS!
I'M TRULY GRATE-FUL, MY FRIEND...

THE POKÉMON LEAGUE WAS QUITE AN INTER-ESTING EVENT.
I HAD THE OPPORTUNITY TO FACE NUMEROUS TRAINERS FROM UNOVA AS WELL AS BATTLE THE ELITE FOUR.

NOT AT ALL.
YOU HELPED ME WITH MY PLANS TOO.

BY ALTERING PEOPLE'S MEMO-RIES, YOU MEAN?

THAT WAS AN INTERESTING PROJECT...
SEVERAL PEOPLE FREED THEIR POKÉMON BECAUSE THEIR MEMORIES HAD BEEN ALTERED BY BEHEEYEM. BUT IT SEEMS THAT OTHERS FREED THEIR POKÉMON BECAUSE THEY WERE PERSUADED BY TEAM PLASMA'S IDEALS.
NEXT, THOSE WHO LACKED CONFIDENCE IN THEIR BONDS WITH THEIR POKÉMON BEGAN FREEING THEIR POKÉMON.
I HOPE TO MAINTAIN THIS FRIENDLY ALLIANCE BETWEEN US.
GLADLY. AS LONG AS YOU DON'T INTERFERE WITH MY RESEARCH.
AS A MATTER OF FACT...
...OUR ALLIANCE WILL BE A BOON TO ME AS WELL...
...FOR I AM RESEARCHING HOW TO...
...BRING OUT THE MAXIMUM POWER OF POKÉMON!
THAT IS *MY* ULTIMATE GOAL!!

YOU HAVE TO GET READY TO GO. WE CAN'T STAY HERE ANYMORE.

WHY CAN'T I STAY WITH THEM, MOMMY?
THESE POKÉMON HAVE ALL BEEN FREED FROM BAD PEOPLE.
THEY'RE MASTER N'S SPECIAL FRIENDS.

NO ...
OF COURSE.

CON-CORDIA!
ANTHEA!

THANK YOU SO MUCH FOR TAKING CARE OF THESE POKÉMON.
WHICH OF THE POKÉMON IS YOUR BEST FRIEND?
HMM ...

THIS ONE!

THEN I WANT YOU TO KEEP IT.
TAKE THIS TOO.
A... PEN-DANT?

IT'S MASTER N'S...!
TAKE GOOD CARE OF IT UNTIL HE RETURNS, OKAY?

TO BE CONTINUED...

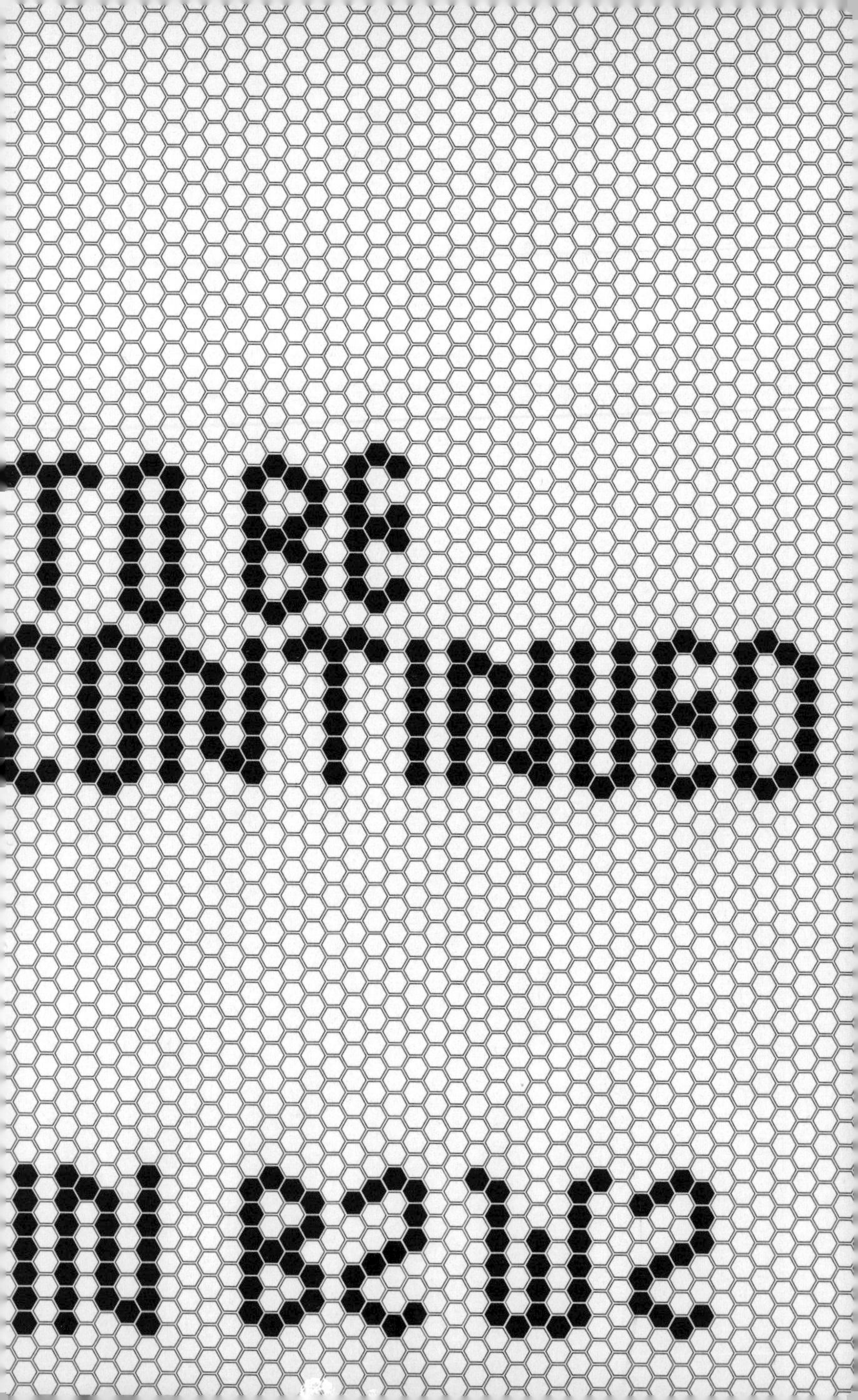
TO BE
CONTINUED

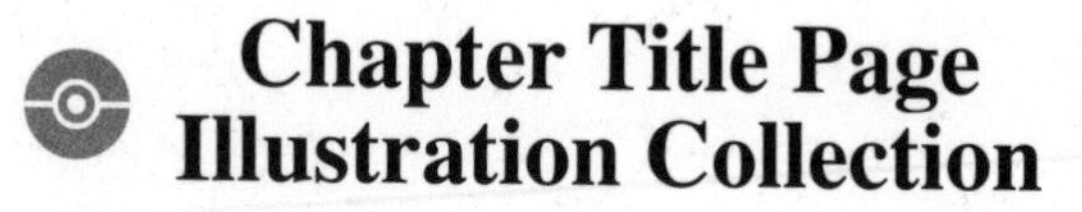

Chapter Title Page Illustration Collection

Presenting title page illustrations originally drawn for some of the chapters of *Pokémon Black & White* when they were first published in Japanese children's magazines *Pokémon Fan* and *Corocoro Ichiban!*

Let's take a look back at Black and White's journey in pictures...

Corocoro Ichiban!
September 2012 Issue

Corocoro Ichiban!
October 2012 Issue

Pokémon Fan
Issue 21

Pokémon Fan
Issue 22

Corocoro Ichiban!
November 2012 Issue

Corocoro Ichiban!
December 2012 Issue

Corocoro Ichiban!
January 2013 Issue

Corocoro Ichiban!
February 2013 Issue

Corocoro Ichiban!
March 2013 Issue

Pokémon Fan
Issue 26

Pokémon Fan
Issue 28

Corocoro Ichiban!
May 2013 Issue

Corocoro Ichiban!
June 2013 Issue

Pokémon Fan
Issue 27

Corocoro Ichiban!
July 2013 Issue

POKÉMON
ADVENTURES
BLACK 2 WHITE 2
vol.
1
DURING THE DAY, HE'S A RICH PLAYER...
YOU SMELL SO NICE, MAYA! IT MUST BE THANKS TO YOUR COMBEE'S HONEY.
So soothing...
HEY, YUKO! DID YOU STYLE YOUR HAIR TO LOOK LIKE YOUR SUNKERN TODAY?
THANKS, GIRLS!
grr
grr
YUKI, YOU'RE AS LIVELY AS THE FLAPPING WINGS OF A WINGULL. BEING AROUND YOU GIVES ME POSITIVE ENERGY!
A NEW STORY ARC!
OOOOH, RACHEL!
HURRY! THE CLASSROOM FOR OUR AFTERNOON CLASS HAS BEEN CHANGED TO ROOM 401!
WE'VE GOT A NEW TEA-CHER!
BUT BY NIGHT... HE'S A TOUGH POKÉMON BATTLER!

A SPECIAL SCHOOL FOR POKÉMON TRAINERS ...

HE'S ALSO A MASTER OF...

POKÉMON BATTLES, POKÉMON CAPTURING, AND POKÉMON EVERY-THING ELSE! IN OTHER WORDS, HE'S... MR. PERFECT!

A BRAND-NEW STORY ARC SET IN THE UNOVA REGION TWO YEARS AFTER THE EVENTS THAT JUST UNFOLDED!

POKÉMON™ ADVENTURES BLACK 2 WHITE 2

FULL THROTTLE AHEAD FOR MORE MYSTERY AND... ROMANCE!

Message from
Hidenori Kusaka

When I was preparing for this story arc and found out the title would be *Black & White*, I tried to come up with black-and-white things that are familiar to kids, who are our main readers, to focus on. We came up with the idea of bar codes and QR codes, systems for reading information. That was what I based my character Black upon. It feels like I created this character ages ago, but at the same time like it was only yesterday. It's time for him to "read" the latest input and make his final deduction. I always feel like this at the end of a story arc...

Message from
Satoshi Yamamoto

My dream in high school was to be able to watch Japanese F/X, action movies and TV shows from the early days up till 1974 at home whenever I wanted to. That dream came true within ten years or so. Let's see if Black's dream comes true too. What will happen to the characters whose dreams come true and those whose dreams do not? This story of dreams, the *Black & White* story arc, is about to come to an end...

Pokémon ADVENTURE
BLACK AND WHIT
Volume
Perfect Square Editi

Story by HIDENORI KUSAK
Art by SATOSHI YAMAMOT

Translation/Tetsuichiro Miy
English Adaptation/Annette Rom
Touch-up & Lettering/Susan Daigle-Le
Design/Shawn Carr
Editor/Annette Rom

Printed in the U.S

Published by VIZ Media,
P.O. Box 77
San Francisco, CA 94

10 9 8 7 6 5 4 3
First printing, October 2

www.perfectsquare.com

www.viz.com

Begin your Pokémon Adventure here in the Kanto region!

RED & BLUE BOX SET

Story by HIDENORI KUSAKA Art by MATO

Includes POKÉMON ADVENTURES Vols. 1-7 and a collectible poster!

All your favorite Pokémon game characters jump out of the screen into the pages of this action-packed manga!

Red doesn't just want to train Pokémon, he wants to be their friend too. Bulbasaur and Poliwhirl seem game. But independent Pikachu won't be so easy to win over!

And watch out for Team Rocket, Red... They only want to be your enemy!

Start the adventure today!